Glad To Be
Insane

First edition January 2019
Published independently

© 2019 Nia Greenwood

All rights reserved

Without limiting the rights under copyright reserved above, no part of this publication may be reproduced, stored or introduced into a retrieval system, or transmitted, in any form or by any means (electronic, mechanical, photocopying, recording or otherwise), without the prior written permission of the author.

ISBN : 9781795506830

Glad To Be Insane

Nia Greenwood

Table of contents

Glad to be insane 1
The Game..17
Blaze..33
Fairytale of York..47
The Top 69
Martha 81
insomnia 87
They 95
Hand in Hand 103
Five Stages 119
Another Girl 129
A Bird...137
Forget 147
Waiting..177

Glad to be insane

"Don't talk to me like that, don't you have any idea what it's been like for me?"

"Yes, actually. We've heard exactly what you think, over and over and over. But did you ever think that maybe . . ."

I turned up the volume on the music that was playing on the radio to try and drown out the sound of arguing. I shoved my brush down into the pot harder and continued mixing Heidi's colour.

"Terri's back then?" she asked.

"By the sounds of it," I replied.

"Why can't she just leave your Dads alone? I can kinda see why Toby left her, no offence or anything though."

"Nah, I get it," I sighed as I dipped my fingers in the mixture and ran them through Heidi's hair. "She's been coming back a lot more lately, drunk quite a lot of the time."

"So I've heard."

There was a silence and I carried on applying blonde to Heidi's hair. The silence was broken by a slightly muffled voice from under a pile of papers on my floor.

"Yo, can I come up please?"

Heidi chuckled.

"Oh, sorry, Archie," I said, lifting all the papers off him. He sat up, grumbling under his breath. I helped him up and he stood, brushing himself off. He looked at the newly applied blonde highlights going through Heidi's normally brown hair. A small smile worked its way across his face.

"Lookin' good." He grinned and Heidi giggled, then his smile faded and I could tell he was trying to listen to something. I sighed. I knew exactly what - or rather who he was eavesdropping on.

"Before you say anything, yes, Terri's here," I said.

Archie held up his hands and looked offended.

"Wasn't gonna say nothin'."

"You were thinking it though," Heidi said.

Archie opened his mouth as though he was going to reply, then he shut it and smirked.

"Can't argue with you now can I, Princess?"

"Awe!" Heidi blushed and I looked away so neither of them would see me cringing.

"No, you don't understand. That weren't a compliment, you're just too stubborn."

I laughed at that, despite myself, and Heidi stuck her tongue out at Archie.

"I love having you two here," I said, laughing. "Takes my mind off the bastards downstairs."

The two of them exchanged a glance as I realised I'd said the last bit out loud.

"I . . . I didn't mean that. I love them, you know I do."

A sly smile crept up on Archie's face.

"What, even Terri?" he asked.

I was silent for a moment as my brain processed what he'd said. Then I came to my senses. I smiled, then a little laugh escaped. Before I knew it the three of us had completely forgotten about everything, including why we were laughing.

After another half hour full of jokes from Archie, and giggles from the two of us I was done with Heidi's hair. I stood back and admired my work.

"There, I think you're done now."

"Oh thanks!" Heidi hugged me after seeing it in the mirror.

"It looks lovely," Archie murmured.

I could see the way he was looking at her, so I decided to get it over with for him. I put my hand on his back and pushed him towards Heidi. They were both shocked for a second before Archie put his arms around Heidi. She relaxed into him and there was a moment of calm as the two of them hugged. I smiled, it was a nice contrast from the constant arguing that had been happening most of the past month or so.

The moment was ruined by an odd feeling spreading throughout me, and an image of me shoving Heidi into the wall and turning to Archie, who was screaming at me. I blinked to try and get rid of it. That couldn't happen now, of all times.

"You have to go now," I said, too quickly.

"What?" Heidi pulled away from Archie.

"I . . . I have homework. And . . . you know, I'll never be able to do it being distracted by you now, will I?" I tried to laugh to make it seem like I was joking.

"Can't it wait?" Archie begged.

"No!" I realised my tone was a little harsh and tried to soften it. "No, it's quite long. I'd better get it done sooner than later."

They sighed.

"Okay then, see you." Heidi mumbled. She gave me a half wave and they trudged back towards their frame. Archie helped Heidi up then followed her himself. Heidi sat in the chair, her back facing towards me and Archie put his hand on her shoulder, looking down into her eyes. They froze.

I sighed and lifted the frame down from the easel. I put it in my cupboard with all the others. Remembering the weird feeling I'd had when Heidi and Archie were hugging, I rooted around and picked out a fresh canvas. The white of the canvas against the dark spruce of the easel was beautiful on its own, but I knew that I was going to create something even more so.

I dipped my brush in the peach paint, mixing it with lots of water to make it light enough. My hand hovered above the canvas as I hesitated; if I did this wrong I'd be stuck with it forever. But the feeling from earlier brought me back to reality. I would do this right and I wouldn't give up. I traced a rough oval on the paper with my brush - the perfect head shape - and started filling it in different shades.

Before long a nose started to emerge, then a mouth, then using the green paint some eyes started to appear. It was like watching someone else paint, like my hand wasn't in my control and just painting whatever it felt like. Time passed twice as fast as it should have, like it always did when I was painting. I moved down to the body, a grey hoodie over a navy t-shirt, and jeans to roughly match. Black socks covered his feet instead of shoes - I could give him some of those later.

I was just shading his clothes to make him look a bit more realistic when I heard Toby calling my name, telling me that tea was ready. I sighed. The paint was so much easier to mix when it was wet, and if I left it too long then I wouldn't be able to make it realistic enough when I got back.

"One second," I called. I hastily finished off all the shadows before stepping back to admire my work. It wasn't perfect, but I could always tweak it slightly when I had more time. I'd done all the bits I needed to do now.

Downstairs Toby and Mike were waiting for me. Laid out on the table they were sitting at were three plates, each with a meal of chicken nuggets and chips, one for me, one for Mike and one for Toby.

"Hey there!" Mike gestured for me to sit down. "School okay today?"

I nodded, chewing on a bit of chicken longer than I needed to avoid having to say anything.

"I haven't seen you downstairs very often lately," Toby said. "What've you been doing up there?"

"Painting. Nothing much."

"Ah, another one of your famed window views?"

"No, I've started doing people."

"Ah, cool. Anyone in particular?"

"They're made up," I snapped. "Why does it even matter?"

I felt a twinge of guilt as the two of them exchanged a glance, but I didn't let it show. Mike reached out to my hand and I pulled away.

"I know things haven't been the easiest lately," Toby started, "but we really are trying our best—"

"You're not *trying*," I said, standing up. "There's no restraining order on the drunk arse who keeps showing up screaming in your faces. I haven't seen Mike making that much of an effort to get a better job even though he keeps saying he will. And neither of you even have any time to talk to me, so I don't know why you're pointing out that you don't see me downstairs because even if I was, you wouldn't take any notice."

"I . . ." Toby faltered, and I knew I'd hit a weak spot.

I picked up my plate and headed for the door.

"Gem, wait," Mike called, but I ignored him and left the room.

Back in the safety of my room, I tried to add more detail to my latest painting through my blurry eyes. I was wiping them furiously with the back of my hands for the third time when I heard a voice.

"Hey, are you okay?"

I looked up to see a boy my age with the ashy brown hair and green eyes of my painting.

"Yeah, I'm fine."

"Really? Because people always tend to say that when all they really want is a good talk and a hug."

"It's . . . complicated."

"I got time." He paused then stood up and held out his hand. "Come on, let's go."

"Where?"

"I don't know, you know this place, you decide."

I thought for a second, then nodded and led him out of my room and down the stairs. We walked past the kitchen where Toby and Mike were talking.

"We're going out," I called and I heard Toby call my name just as I closed the front door behind us.

I led the boy down roads, through a park, into the trees and along winding paths so familiar I could've walked them with my eyes closed. We arrived at a clearing surrounded by trees and sat down on a bench overlooking a small pond speckled with sunlight that was just peeking through the leaves above.

"Spill," he said.

"Woah, hold on. We don't even know each other yet."

"True." He laughed. "And I don't even know myself."

"Exactly," I said, carrying on so that I didn't have to talk about my feelings. "So who are you then? Who do you feel like?"

He tilted his head as if he was trying to remember something. "Faolàn . . . I like that name. And I'm probably about fifteen. I don't have much else I can say about myself."

"Well let's invent you a story then."

"I'm not all that creative," Faolàn admitted. "Tell me about yourself first so that I have some inspiration."

I laughed bitterly. "You don't want inspiration from my life, trust me."

"Try me."

I sighed. "Okay. My name is Gem. I'm fifteen years old and I live with my two adoptive Dads, Toby and Mike. Toby's ex girlfriend, Terri, is really homophobic, and she keeps coming to our house drunk and barely sane, screaming things about how her life has been ruined since Toby left her and how it's disgusting and abnormal that he married another man. My only two friends are in love, and sometimes I feel like I'm third-wheeling, and that they don't appreciate that they wouldn't even know each other if it wasn't for me. And I have this thing where I can't control my imagination, and I see myself doing horrible things to people, and sometimes I actually do." I choked. I'd been talking too fast and now tears were running down my face.

"Hey." Faolàn put his arms around my shoulders. "I know I can't sort anything out but most of this is just how you're feeling, and maybe if you looked at it differently it wouldn't seem so bad."

"What d'you mean?" I mumbled.

"Well, do Terri's opinions really matter? If she doesn't like gay people then that's her problem, what matters is what your Dads and the people who are important think. Secondly, a third wheel isn't completely useless. Think of it this way - a bike can't stand on its own, it needs some external support or else it'll just fall down. A trike, on the other hand, is perfectly stable, and all because it has the help of that extra wheel. You get what I'm trying to say?"

I nodded and smiled despite myself.

"So what about you then?"

"Yes, my story."

We spent a while writing a backstory for Faolàn until it started getting dark and I decided that it was about time I apologised to Toby and Mike.

"Let's go back," I said, standing up and leading him back the way we came, until we arrived at the house. I pulled out the key I always kept in my pocket and unlocked the door for us to go in.

"You'd better go up," I told Faolàn. "This could be awkward." He nodded and ran upstairs, and I went to find my Dads. It wasn't hard. Mike was sitting at the computer - browsing available jobs.

"Mike," I practically whispered, "you're actually looking."

Mike turned and smirked. "Don't sound so surprised, young lady." He held out his arms and I ran to him, grateful he wasn't bitter about earlier.

"You're back," Toby's voice came from behind me.

I turned and nodded sheepishly.

"Are you okay?"

I nodded again. "Yeah, sorry about earlier."

Toby sighed. "It's fine. You had a point too." He laughed softly. "Although . . . "

"What?"

"Don't use language like that in my house again please." I nodded, relieved that it was only that. Then he held out his arms and I hugged him too.

"Gem," Toby said when we'd pulled apart. "One thing that's been bothering me."

"Yeah?"

"When you left, you said 'we're going out'. We. As in more than one person. Who was with you?"

I shrugged, trying to sound as casual as possible when really my heart was thudding against my ribcage. "Slip of the tongue I guess." I felt my face flushing, and desperately tried to think of any excuse to leave the room. "I'm going back upstairs. I want to finish my painting before the paint is too dry."

I dashed out before either of them could say anything, and shut myself back in my room. I slid down the door until I was sitting on the floor, breathing hard. I'd done that before, but this was the first time anyone had picked up on it.

Faolàn was standing in his frame again. "How'd it go?"

"Great," I lied, taking a deep breath. "Anyway. I have someone for you to meet."

He watched as I opened the wardrobe and lifted Heidi and Archie's frame out. Heidi turned around from where she'd been sitting with her back turned to us, taking to Archie.

"Oh hey!" She smiled. Then she saw Faolàn. "Who's this?"

"This is Faolàn," I said. "Heidi, and Archie." I pointed to the appropriate person as I said their names.

"Nice to . . . " Archie tailed off as there was a door slamming downstairs and the sound of shouting. His eyes widened as we all heard a set of loud footsteps coming up the stairs.

"Quick, go," I hissed, ushering everyone back into their frames.

The door banged open and Terri burst in, eyes wild, a wicked grin on her face.

"Who were you talking to, girl?" she snarled.

I gulped. "Nobody."

"Don't lie to me again. I heard you."

I shook my head, I didn't trust my voice enough to speak.

"Hm. Never mind. I came up here because of something your *Dads* told me." She spat the word 'Dads' like it was a bad taste in her mouth. "What's this idea about a restraining order huh?"

I couldn't answer. Terri moved closer to me, breathing heavily. Her breath stank of whiskey and cigarette smoke, and I resisted the desperate urge to cough.

"Is that how bad I really am?" she fake-sobbed. "Am I such a bad person that you want to ban me from ever coming near here?" She blinked rapidly and pretended to hold back tears.

I wanted to scream *What do you think?* I wanted to tell her exactly how much I hated her guts and never wanted to see her ever again. I wanted to say that homophobia is not okay and that she's much more disgusting than two men being in love. I wanted to tell her so much, but just the sight of her sent my brain into jelly mode, completely useless and more likely to make things worse than solve them.

"Clear off would you!"

I turned to see Faolàn standing by my side.

"What are you doing?" I hissed.

Terri looked between me and Faolàn's frame.

"What is this?" she laughed menacingly. "You're talking to your paintings?"

"N-no," I stammered. I would have given Faolàn a death stare but I couldn't take my eyes off the unstable woman in front of me.

"You are!" She cackled. "Oh, and they call *me* insane!" She reached forward and grabbed Faolàn's frame, with him inside. She held it up to her face and stared him in the eyes.

"What have you been saying to the little girl then? What have you been doing that's made her like this to me?"

"It's not him, it's you," I blurted.

Terri turned to me. "What?"

I took a deep breath. "It's not his fault I don't like you," I repeated calmly. "It's just you."

"You, you little . . ."

"Little what?" I demanded. "Come on, spit it out, Terri. I'm sure we'd all like to know what you think, after all, your opinion is always so *valued*."

I regretted it as soon as I'd said it. Terri's eyes turned fiery, an anger I'd only ever seen once before, in Toby when Terri first came to the house. She took a step forward and grabbed the nearest thing - which just happened to be Heidi's frame. Heidi squeaked in terror.

"Put her down!" I demanded, my voice coming out stronger than I felt.

"Her?" Terri's laugh was that of a madwoman. "Her? This is an inanimate object, an *it*. It doesn't have feelings. It doesn't live." She lifted the frame high above her head. "You're just as abnormal as your Dads!"

Everything happened in slow-motion then. Terri brought the frame down and it crashed over my head. I'd barely registered what had happened before I collapsed to the floor.

•••

As I came to, I could tell immediately that this wasn't my room. I was in a strange bed in a strange room in a strange building. The air smelled of sanitiser and rubber gloves, and everything was so clean and shiny it made my eyes hurt. I tried to think where I was, to remember what happened to lead to me being here now.

Suddenly I remembered it all. Terri came to the house, she smashed Heidi's frame. Heidi . . . she's gone.

Stop it, I told myself. *She wasn't ever real*.

I didn't have to wait long before someone came into the room. A woman in a pressed white uniform pushed open the door and came to sit next to my bed.

"Hello, Gem," she said. "I'm Doctor Miller."

"A doctor?" Everything started to sink in. I rubbed my forehead, which felt like it was burning.

"I'm afraid we had to sedate you to get you here," Doctor Miller continued, "so you'll probably be feeling a bit rough for a little while."

"What?" My voice was barely a whisper. "Why?"

"Well, you weren't keen on the idea of coming here. If we hadn't you could've hurt someone, or yourself."

I get it, I thought to myself. *She's calling me insane*.

"And where is 'here'?"

"I'm afraid you're at the hospital. The psychiatric ward."

So she's not just calling me insane, I actually am. My breath sped up and I felt the tell-tale tingle in the corner of my eye. Everything was ruined now. My life at home with Toby and Mike, although it wasn't the best, was one of the few things in life that mattered to me. My two best friends, one of them was gone forever, and the other I'd have to wait for goodness knows how long to see again. And Faolàn, we'd only just met but we were getting along so perfectly. Now that I thought about it he was right. If I'd stopped being so negative, life would have been so much better.

"I want to talk about some of the things you shouted at your house before we sedated you," Doctor Miller said, interrupting my thoughts. "You mentioned a Heidi, that Terri had killed her. What's this about? As far as we know Terri hasn't done anything of the sort."

I sighed. "Heidi isn't real," I mumbled. "She's a painting that Terri smashed. I used to talk to her, I talked to all my painted people."

"Might there have been an Archie too?"

I nodded, wiping at my cheeks which were now wet.

"You realise this isn't normal, right?"

I nodded again. She was trying to be nice about it, which I had to admire. I couldn't have thought how to put something like this nicely.

"I just want to help you."

"I know."

"I'm not here to scare you, that's not my job. I'm here to tell you the truth and help you get your head around it."

"And what is the truth?" I stared deep into her eyes, challenging her to say it.

"You've had a troubled past. It seems that has affected your mental health and so you're seeing things that aren't real."

"So I'm insane." I said, surprised at how calm I sounded.

"Not necessarily."

I sighed. Adults, they're always coming up with ways to dodge the truth, never actually telling you what they're thinking.

"With the right treatment and input from the both of us, you could go back to your old life."

It sounded great, but it would never be the same without Heidi, Archie and Faolàn. I nodded anyway, and agreed to tell her anything that came into my head.

•••

After a couple of weeks pretending I'm not seeing anything and telling everyone I feel fine, I'm allowed to go back home. Doctor Miller suggested I don't go straight to my room as it might bring back memories, but that's exactly what I do. Heidi's frame has been tidied away, and Archie's is back in my wardrobe. I pick it up and trace the outside of his body with my finger, knowing that I'll never be able to talk to him again.

Then Faolàn's frame catches my eye. It is completely blank. Faolàn is nowhere to be seen; it's like he stood up and walked off, even though I remind myself that that's impossible. Surely.

"Hey, Gem."

I turn to see him, standing behind me. He looks just as perfect as ever, and better because I hadn't expected we'd ever be in this position again.

"How do you feel now?" he asks. "Who are you?"

I smile. "My name is Gem, I'm fifteen years old and I live with my two adoptive Dads." I step towards him. "And my life has never been better."

He pulls me in a tight embrace. "My name is Faolàn," he whispers in my ear. "I'm fifteen years old and I'm hugging the girl of my dreams. My life has never been better."

We stand there for a while, arms around each other, my head resting in the side of his neck. And I know that whatever has happened, or is going to happen in the future, that in this precise moment, I'm glad to be insane.

The Game

She makes another jab with her sword. I dive to the ground and roll away just in time, standing up and blocking yet another blow with my own. Backing away a bit, I grip my sword with both hands and get ready for her to strike again. She does, being the predictable person she is, and I lift my sword to greet hers. The scraping of metal on metal fills the air for a second, and with one sweeping motion I knock her sword out of her hand, sending it skidding across the floor. I then place mine on her shoulder, inches away from her face which is filled with fear. Her eyes meet mine, and for a moment she looks defeated.

With one flick of her wrist an invisible force knocks into me, sending me flying backwards. She takes this opportunity to pick up her sword and stand up straight again. She brushes herself off, and smirks.

"Hey, that's cheating," I wheeze. "Swords only, no powers. That was the rule. I might have actually beaten you otherwise."

Faith shrugs. "You could never beat me." She says it even though she knows I could. Sword fighting is the only thing I'm better at than her, the only thing I'm even good at to be honest. She just can't admit it. It's not possible for someone to be better than Faith.

She helps me to my feet and we sheath our swords. Steph and Theo come running over.

"That was really cool," Steph says. "When can we have a go?"

Faith and I glance at each other and I wait for her to come up with an excuse for why they can't yet. They don't realise that the swords are real and sharp, and if they do they don't understand quite how much damage they could do if they make a mistake.

"Powers are more useful," Faith explains. "They're long-distance and can do more harm that you could ever do with a sword. Plus, they're more dangerous if you can't use them properly."

Steph's face falls, but a grin spreads back across it as Theo speaks.

"What if we're on a quest, and there are loads of people surrounding us with swords and the easiest way to fight them is to use a sword?" He shakes his arm around as he talks like he's brandishing a sword.

Faith rolls her eyes. "Let's think about that when it comes, eh?" She takes the two of them by their shoulders and they walk off together, leaving me with the swords. I take them back to the shed where we keep them and follow the others into the house.

•••

He was walking along the corridor, minding his own business when she came running up to him. She was out of breath but he could still sense her excitement.

"Finally, I found you!"

Before he had a chance to ask her what she meant she'd dragged him through the nearest door, which just happened to be the cloakroom. Once inside, she pushed him up against the far wall.

"What the—"

"Shh!" She held a finger up to her lips and looked around, as if checking that nobody else was there. It was then that he recognised her. She was in his class, although he couldn't remember her name. She was a bit strange, he knew that. She also didn't seem to have many other friends. He could only guess what she was doing now. They'd never talked before, so what did she want with him?

"This is going to sound super crazy," she said.

"It already is."

"Okay so, I can do things, and I don't mean, like, normal things."

"So what do you mean?"

"I can make things happen. With my mind."

"Yeah, right." He couldn't see where this conversation was going, but he didn't like it at the moment.

"I'm serious. And it's okay if you don't believe me but I think you might be the same."

He stared at her. She seemed so serious, like she actually believed what she was saying. "The same?"

"As in, like me." She tailed off at the end and hung her head, as if she knew how stupid it sounded.

"Prove it."

"Wh-what?"

"Prove it," he repeated, slowly and clearly. *"Prove you can . . . 'do things'."*

He crossed his arms and gave her 'the look'. It was something his mother always did when she wanted the truth out of him, and he'd always wanted to use it on someone else. The girl hung her head.

"I can't. Not here."

He scoffed and pushed past her. "I'll bet you can't," he muttered under his breath. "Do things, how thick do you think I am?"

He didn't give her a chance to answer, knowing that she wouldn't anyway. Instead, he left her there, standing in amongst all the coats like a little lost child.

•••

Steph's fireball hits into the target with a sickening crack. It leans back slightly as the flames eat it up, turning it black and hard before it disintegrates into nothingness. Faith pauses, shocked for a second before she starts clapping.

"That was good. Try aiming more towards the bottom next time, you know, since fire travels upwards and all."

Steph sighs as Faith waves her hand and the black dusty remains of the target pull together to rebuild the wooden soldier Steph was aiming for, but she tries again all the same. She plants her feet firmly in the ground, and with one swift movement she moves her hands forward like she's pushing something and another fireball erupts from her palms, shooting straight to the target's support. The whole thing catches fire immediately and disappears.

"That was better," Faith congratulates her.

"Yeah, amazing. My turn now," Theo says hurriedly, as Steph wanders off somewhere I don't see.

"Uh, yeah sure." Faith waves her hand again and the target reappears, while Theo stands where Steph had been. He clenches his fists and stares at the target, before punching the air in front of him. The target explodes. Unfortunately so does a nearby tree. When the smoke clears all that remains is the smouldering base of the trunk and some fried leaves. Theo sighs.

"I can never get it right, can I?"

While Faith goes over to comfort him, somebody taps my shoulder. I turn to face Steph, a worried expression on her face.

"What?" I ask.

"I-I'm not sure how to say it, I . . ."

"Steph, calm down," I say, as tears start shining in her eyes. I take her round the side of Faith's house where we're out of sight of the others.

"Sorry, Kit," she says. "I didn't mean to get like this. It's just that my Dad lost his job a while back, and he can't seem to get another. We've been a bit short on money for a while, but now it won't be long before we can't afford to keep renting our house, so . . . we're moving." She spits the last bit out like she'd been holding it in her mouth too long, which she probably had, in a way.

"What?" I almost don't believe she just said it. My mind must be making me hear things. Except, it's not. Steph really is moving away.

"We're moving house. To an area where houses are cheaper, and maybe we'll only get a flat. Dad has an interview for a job next week. In Canton."

"But that's ages away. You'll have to move to a different school, and . . ."

Steph nods slowly. "That's my point."

I pause before asking my next question.

"Why are you telling me?"

"Wh-what d'you mean?"

"I mean, why are you telling *me* rather than Faith or Theo?"

"Well, they're both busy." She looks down at her hands which are clasped in her lap for a moment. "And I think I trust you the most."

I reach out hesitantly, and awkwardly put my hand on her shoulder in an attempt to console her. I'm not really sure what to do in these situations, and I don't know what would make Steph feel better. She stands up and hugs me, and I hug her back, stiffly. I'm not that keen on people touching me, but Steph needs the reassurance so I let her.

"Promise you won't tell them?" she whispers. "Not yet, anyway. I want them to hear it from me."

I nod. "Promise."

The calm is broken by Faith's loud voice.

"Well, what's happening here then?" She sounds annoyed, and when I turn to her I see she looks it too.

"I—" I break off as I try to think of something so as not to tell them. "Steph isn't feeling well," I blurt.

I glance at Steph who gives me a little smile. Her secret is safe. For now.

"Oh," Faith says, a bit put-out. "Well, maybe you'd better go home then." Faith takes her inside to her Mum, who barely notices the mess in the garden, or if she does, she doesn't mind.

"Will she be okay?" Theo asks after a while.

"Yeah," I say, trying not to give anything away. "She's not too bad."

•••

He was sat on the bench, watching the other boys playing football and trying to work out where the appeal was. They kicked a ball around a field and into a goal, that was all. He didn't understand what they found fun about it. He much preferred sitting here reading, although it'd be much more fun if he had someone to talk to.

As if on cue, the girl who'd cornered him in the cloakroom came bounding up to him.

"Where are your friends?" she asked, and he could detect a slight mocking tone underneath the genuine curiosity. Instead of answering, he just shrugged, which made her ask more.

"Why aren't you playing with the other boys?"

"Don't like football."

"Or the other boys, huh."

He stood up. "What do you want?"

She smiled. "I know exactly what I want, but the question is, what do you *want?"*

He shook his head and sat down again, opening his book. He didn't have the time to waste on her. She carried on anyway.

"I think you want a friend. You're bored here and you want somebody to talk to, or do something with. I can offer that."

She talked about companionship like it was money or a nice holiday that she bribed people with to get them to be her friend in return.

"Come with me," she said, without waiting for his answer. She grabbed his wrist and led him to the back of the playground away from everybody else.

"I don't think anybody can see us here," she whispered. "Anyway, watch this."

She held up her hand and cupped it like she was holding an invisible bowl. For a while, nothing happened, and he was beginning to think this was just wasting his time and he could be doing something more useful, like reading his book. Alone. That thought made him think that maybe it was time he got some friends, so he turned back to the girl. But before he could say anything, he froze on the spot.

A branch from the hedge next to them was slowly bending its way down towards her hand, as if it was being pulled by an imaginary force. I can do things. *He heard her voice from the day before echoing in his head. So this was what she meant. She really could do things with her mind. Then, he remembered something else she'd said.*

"So I can do this too?"

The girl paused and tilted her head like she was thinking. "I'm not sure. I think you're slightly different."

She pulled something out of her pocket and handed it to him. It was a necklace, a round green charm on a black string.

The charm was about the size of a pound coin, with a tree engraved on it.

"What is it?" he asked.

"Your Stone," she replied, grinning. "The power of creation."

• • •

The Stone is cold against my chest as I hide it underneath my school shirt. It's what I do every morning; the others do the same. We have to hide them when we go to school. It's not like the weekends when we're at Faith's house, where we can keep them out and not worry about anybody breaking them or anything.

I wonder if Steph will tell Theo and Faith about her moving soon. I'm not very good at keeping things from people, especially Faith. If she realises something is up she'll ask, and I'll most likely fold and tell her. I make a mental note to remind Steph as soon as I see her in school.

But I don't find her. She isn't there at the start of the day when I normally meet my friends, and by breaktime I still haven't seen her.

"Have you seen Steph?" I ask Faith and Theo at break, as casually as I can.

"No," Theo says. "Have you?"

I shake my head and resist the urge to say *no, that's why I asked*. Then I realise Faith is studying me.

"What's going on with you two?" she asks.

"What?" I glance at Theo, who looks just as confused as I am.

"You know what I mean. You're always together, whispering and stuff. What's going on?"

"Nothing. And if this is about what happened yesterday, Steph was ill and I was trying to make her feel better."

"Really?"

"Yes!"

"What's your problem, Faith?" Theo says, backing me up. "Why don't you believe him?"

"Well, if Steph really was ill, then surely you wouldn't be asking why she isn't in school today."

"I—" I realise she has a point. "I didn't ask why she wasn't in, I just asked if you'd seen her."

Faith gives me a look and I hope what I've said will be enough to stop her asking any more questions. If she says anything else I may just cave in and blurt it out. Instead, she turns and leaves me and Theo alone, staring after her, not quite believing what just happened.

"What's up with her?" Theo says again.

"Just leave it," I tell him. "She'll get over it. She does this sometimes, but it doesn't take her long to forget."

Theo nods and I only wish it was that easy to convince myself.

●●●

Two weeks later he followed her across the makeshift football pitch the other boys were using and to a bench. She introduced herself as Faith and he introduced himself as Kit.

"I'm Theo," the new boy said. He had a slight Scottish accent and thick rimmed glasses which he had to keep pushing back up his nose.

"I'm Steph," the girl sitting next to him said. "Although you already know that."

Steph was in their class, but Kit didn't remember ever speaking to her before. In fact, that was the case with pretty much everyone in their class. He didn't like people, though being friends with Faith seemed to have given him the confidence to be here talking to these two almost-strangers now.

"Okay let's cut out all the nonsense," Faith said. "We need your help. Both of you."

"What for?" Theo asked, sounding genuinely interested.

"We're going on a quest," Faith explained. "And we need your help."

Steph laughed. "What kind of a quest?" she asked, almost mockingly. "And how would we help?"

Faith pulled two more necklaces out of her pocket. A red one and a brown one. "With these. Here's fire," she said, as she gave the red one to Steph, "and for you, the power of explosions." She handed Theo the brown one. They exchanged a confused glance.

"What's this all about?"

"Like I said, we're going on a quest." Faith pulled out her Stone - a yellow one with a hand engraved on it. "This is mine, telekinesis. Kit here has the power of creation."

Kit pulled his out and showed them.

"We'll need these powers for our quest," she continued. "After you learn how to control them a bit better."

"Sorry," Steph said. "But can I remind you that you're all ten years old, and I'm nine. Even though I'm the youngest I seem to be the only one thinking clearly here. We're not old enough to go on a quest all by ourselves, and even if we did, these things are hardly real." She held her stone up and glared at it.

Faith held out her hand and Steph's Stone went flying into it. She wrapped her fingers around it and smirked.

"Well if you're not coming then I might just go and give this to somebody else."

"Woah, that was cool!" Theo cried. "Did you see that, Steph?"

Steph was speechless.

"Told you they're real," Faith said, grinning even more. She tossed Steph's Stone back to her. "Well, put them on then!"

Steph and Theo did as they were told.

"Let's go test them," Kit suggested.

"Yeah," Steph said. "And get ready for our quest."

● ● ●

At lunch the next day I notice that Faith is a bit quiet, but I don't say anything. I'm too busy trying to silently urge Steph to say something. Even if she gets my message, Theo is distracting her, blabbing on about a quest he wants us to go on.

". . . So then we'll be in this huge room with a throne and everything, and little knights with swords and shields lining the walls. Up ahead along the red carpet is the crown on an altar in front of the throne - the one thousands have died trying to get. And nobody's even managed to touch the crown."

"Why not?" Steph asks, almost as wrapped up in the scene as Theo is.

"Because when we're about ten, fifteen feet away from it, the knights' heads all lift up at the same time, and they run forward and draw their swords, and we have to fight all three hundred and fifty of them off before we can get to the crown. It's almost impossible, but imagine how cool it would be if we're the first people to retrieve the crown."

Steph laughs. "That was in a story, Theo. It's not a real place. And even if it was it'd be too dangerous."

"No it wouldn't. We have our powers. We'd manage, wouldn't we, Kit?"

I'm about to answer when Faith stands up abruptly, slamming her hands down on the table.

"I've had enough of you," she shouts, picking up her lunchbox before storming out.

We're silent for a bit before Steph speaks.

"What was that all about?"

"I don't know," Theo says. "She's been a bit weird since you left her house on Sunday."

"What did you do?"

"Nothing," I say. "Honestly, I can't think of anything."

We stand up simultaneously and go to look for Faith. We check everywhere, but by the time the bell rings telling us to go back to class, we still haven't found her.

"It'll be fine," I tell them. "I sit next to Faith now, I'll talk to her."

It seems to be enough for them, but I have no idea what I'm going to say.

"Are you okay?" seems like a safe bet, so that's what I say when I sit down next to her.

Faith shrugs.

"Come on, tell me. If we've done something we want to know what it is, you know, so we can make things better between us. What's up?"

Faith turns to me suddenly, and I jump slightly. "I'll tell you *what's up*," she snaps. "I started this whole thing. I gave you the Stones and let you have the powers. I know the most about them. All I want in return is a little respect, but they all seem so fond of you nobody pays any attention to me."

"Faith, I—"

"You and Theo are *besties* now, so I see. And if you and Steph don't tell us what's going on then you have no hope of 'making things better between us'. You had no friends at all when I first met you, and now look at you. Steph and Theo adore you, and who's the reason for that? Me! That's who. No thanks, not even a teeny tiny bit of respect for me, after all I've done for you. All of you!" She reaches forward and grabs the Stone from around my neck. She tugs it and the string breaks. "I'll take this. And don't expect to ever go on another quest with me again."

She picks her books and pencil case up and walks over to the teacher. She's probably asking to move because she 'can't concentrate where she is' or some rubbish, because the teacher points to somebody the other side of the class and asks them to swap with Faith. I spend the rest of the lesson sitting next to Judy Walters, who picks her nose constantly and keeps asking me questions about the work.

At afternoon break I'm sitting on the floor at the back of the playground when Steph and Theo come running up to me.

"Faith took your Stone too, did she?" Theo asks.

I nod, not trusting myself to say anything.

"Why though?" Steph says. "What's the point? What's she going to do, bribe us by saying she won't give our powers back until we apologise?"

"She didn't take our powers." I mutter.

"That's so rude, our powers are so cool—"

"She didn't take our powers," I say again, louder this time, and Theo stops talking.

"What d'you mean?"

"Do you have our Stones?" Steph asks, her eyes lighting up. I almost want to say yes rather than what I'm intending to say, just so it'll hurt their feelings less.

"No," I say eventually. "No, I don't have the Stones. What I mean is, Faith couldn't have taken our powers away."

"Why not?"

"Because . . . because we never had any in the first place."

I say it too quickly, like if I get it over with it won't hurt so badly afterwards. Steph and Theo share a confused look and I know I'm wrong. It hurts just as much.

"What?"

"It was all a game, and you know that. We never really had powers."

There's a pause as that information sinks in.

"Yeah," Theo says, breaking the awkward silence. "Yeah. Faith has no right to end our game just because of some stupid argument. It may not have been real, but I still loved it."

"Me too," Steph says, standing up to join Theo, who is already on his feet. "We can play without her. We don't need the stupid Stones."

"And we can go on any quest we like." Theo nods his head determinedly. "We don't need her."

They walk off arm in arm, discussing the next quests they're going to go on in their game. I stay behind, watching them. Steph seems to have forgotten that she's moving, and Theo is still oblivious. I leave them like that; they need to enjoy this time together. I'm glad they took it so well, but part of me still feels like it won't be the same now, even if Faith comes back, because now they know it's all a game. And even though they knew anyway, now that it's been said, that thought will be lingering in the back of their heads, niggling at them no matter what they throw at it, rather than wrapped up in the excitement of having a secret that makes us different from everybody else.

Blaze

His eyes snap open suddenly.

You have to stop yourself from making a sound; you weren't expecting him to wake this soon. You calm yourself and sit back down, eyes focused on the boy. You watch as he stands up and takes in his surroundings - the charred walls, the floorboards that stick up here and there. He walks over to a hole in the wall and looks out over the blackened remains of the house. He sniffs. Clearly the lingering smell of smoke isn't one he likes. You, on the other hand, have always loved the smell of burning wood. You find it comforting, it reminds you of home, of your past and your family . . .

But it's all in the past, you remind yourself. This is now. You turn your attention back to the boy, who's moving about the house, exploring its burnt remains and peeking through its cracked doors. Pressing a couple of buttons on your laptop, you can see the room he's moved to. You lean forwards with curiosity. *Who are you?* you ask him in your head. *How are you alive?*

The boy continues to look around, not a single mark on him. He's completely unscathed, and by the looks of it, completely clueless. You may not have managed to damage him necessarily, but at least his memory has been. He won't be able to remember anything about what happened.

He turns suddenly and stares directly at you.

"Who are you?" he shouts. "What do you want?"

You're taken aback. You weren't expecting him to find your cameras at all, especially not a couple of minutes after he woke. He stares right into your eyes, as if he can see you through the camera's lens. His eyes shimmer as he examines the camera. There's definitely something about him, you decide, and you need to take action, now.

You shut the laptop and, as silently as possible, leave your apartment. You tiptoe down the stairs, making a mental note that if you're going to keep on sneaking out like you have been lately you'll need to get yourself a place of your own. You don't want the neighbours hearing anything and getting suspicious, you can't afford that, not after all the success you've been having recently.

Your car is waiting on the street outside, like it should be. You're always paranoid somebody will steal it since it's old and doesn't always lock. You make another mental note to get a better car, and a job first so that you actually have some money to get a car with. Getting into the seat you place the laptop on the one next to you, and do the one thing you promised yourself when you started that you'd never do.

You're going back to the house.

It doesn't take long to find the boy once you're there. He's standing with his back to you, and you don't know how to call him so you just shout.

"Hey!"

He turns, his eyes fiery, and storms over to you.

"Who are you?" he demands.

"Who are *you*?"

"I asked first."

You sigh. "Kid, look. We can do this as long as you like but you're not going to find out anything about me. Now, I repeat. Who are you?"

He lifts his chin in an attempt to look taller. "No."

"If you won't tell me, then I can't help you."

"Yeah, right."

You shake your head and turn away. You won't waste your energy on a silly little boy. You're about to open what's left of the front door when he speaks again.

"Wait."

You turn back and lean against the door, so that you have an escape if needs must. "I'm listening."

"I . . . what happened?"

You pause and smile slyly. This game is fun.

"Why is everything like this?" he continues.

"Like what?"

"You know what. Why is my house all burnt? Where is my family? Why are you here—?"

"What is your name?"

He looks taken aback for a second. Then he pulls his jacket tighter around his shoulders, straightens up and says, "Jack Goff."

You have to bite your tongue to stop yourself smirking. "Very funny, kid." Turning away, you rack your memory. "Your name is Noah Green. You're twelve years old if I remember correctly."

"Thirteen," he says, like it matters.

"Whatever."

"What d'you mean when you say 'if I remember correctly'?"

"I mean, if my memory is still working and what it tells me is true."

He rolls his eyes and you find yourself rather enjoying tormenting him.

"You know what I mean. How do you know me?"

"I've been watching you." The words are out of your mouth before you can stop them, and you decide that you might as well tell the boy everything. He deserves to know, seeing as he won't make it through the night.

"Come with me," you say. "You can ask any question you want then."

You turn and push away the only part of the front door that's left and make your way down the front steps, avoiding the gaps and the bits which look like they could give way and swallow up your foot within seconds. The car is still outside, and you find yourself relaxing a bit. At least one part of your plan is going well.

"Oh no," Noah says. "I'm not going anywhere with you."

You sigh. "Kid, listen. You have nobody. Your parents are dead, and your house is going to collapse any minute. Everybody else is asleep, so what choice do you have?"

"They . . . they're dead?"

Tears shine in his eyes and you roll yours. You'd thought he would've worked it out by now.

"Get in the car," you say, opening the door. You don't understand emotions, you never did.

The journey is a silent one, apart from the occasional sniffle from the crying child in the backseat. You don't say anything to comfort him; you have nothing. He doesn't ask for it either, just sits there feeling sorry for himself. When you finally reach your apartment, he's been completely silent for a while. You pull the car up against the pavement and get out to open his door.

Angry brown eyes stare up at you when you look down. They shimmer faintly, and you find yourself slightly unnerved. You brush it off, telling yourself he's just been crying, and hold out your hand, gesturing for him to get out. For a while he doesn't move, and you consider shutting the door and locking him in there. Then he stands up suddenly and stalks over to the door of the apartment building. You sigh and follow him, unlocking the door and letting him in.

"Be very quiet," you hiss, holding a finger up to your lips. He rolls his eyes and follows you up the stairs, always putting his feet down a little too hard, just to spite you.

You open the front door to your apartment and let him into the little lobby. He stands tapping his foot impatiently as you lock the first door and fumble with the keys before turning to open the second. As soon as you've opened the door he strides in and stands in the middle of the room.

"Well, find a seat, then," you say, as you turn and see him standing there awkwardly. He kicks a few bits and pieces around on the floor, and for the first time you notice that your place could really do with a good clean. You flick the light switch and light floods the room, allowing the boy to find a half-decent chair and slump down in it.

"My uncle's a police officer," he says.

"Good for him," you mutter, turning to the area of the room you've designated as a kitchen to make yourself a coffee. You're going to need the energy to stay up, otherwise the boy could change his mind and run.

"He could have you arrested."

"That's nice." You take a sip and sit down on a chair near enough to Noah's, in between him and the door. "And how exactly are you going to contact this uncle of yours? Write a letter? Phone him?"

"I . . ." He tails off as he realises you have a point.

"And even if you do get hold of him, how is he going to know where to find you?"

Noah doesn't answer.

"So. You have all night to ask anything you want, and I promise to answer every question truthfully."

He eyes you skeptically. "Promise?"

You nod.

"Who are you?"

"My name is Blaze."

"Bit ironic."

"I know. That's why I chose it."

He tilts his head and gives you a confused look. "So it's not your real name?"

"Oh it's my real name all right, it just wasn't always my name."

Noah shakes his head and tries another. "What happened to my house?"

You sigh. "Ah, that."

"Remember, you'll answer every question truthfully."

"Yes. It burned down."

Noah rolls his eyes. "Well thanks, I hadn't noticed. No, I mean, how? Why?"

"How?" You decide to be blunt with him. "I set it on fire."

"You what?" He gets up out of his chair, towering over you. "What is wrong with you? You don't just go around burning people's houses. That's sick. You're sick. My parents are dead because of you."

"I know, and you should be too."

He stops for a second. "What?"

"You should have burned in that fire like your parents. You shouldn't be here. If you'd just died with them like a good little boy then you wouldn't need to feel like this. You'd be dead too, and you wouldn't miss them."

"So why aren't I?"

"I don't know. Somehow you're completely fine."

"Oh." He sits back down.

"What do you remember?"

"I'm supposed to be the one asking questions."

"But now I am. What do you remember from before you woke up?"

"I don't know. I was asleep and the smell of burning woke me. I think I tried to call for somebody. That's all I can remember." He looks sad, then he stands up again and you're surprised again by his sudden changes in emotions.

"Why did you do it?" he says, his voice shaking. "Why did you burn my house? *Why did you kill them*?"

"It's a long story," you say, surprised at how calm your voice comes out.

"I've got time. Like you said, I have all night. And you were going to answer every question truthfully."

You sigh. Damn this child and his memory.

"That one's an exception to the rules. All I'll say is that when I was about your age - twelve or thirteen - my house caught fire while we were sleeping. I managed to escape but I lost my mother, my father, and my two sisters, all because of something as stupid and natural as fire."

Noah is silent for a moment. Then he shakes his head. "That's no excuse. I lost my mother and father today too, but because of you. And I didn't even have any connection with the fire that killed your family—"

"Shut it, kid," you snap suddenly. "Or I'll bloody well throw you out in the cold." You gesture to the window and the boy looks out over the street, which is now covered in a thin layer of flaky snow.

"I survived the fire. What's to say I can't survive out there?"

"Snow isn't as dangerous."

"So why throw me out?"

He's right. That didn't make sense. None of your thoughts seem to work.

"Look, you're not special, kid. It was a mistake, okay? You survived by accident."

Noah shrugs and walks over to the desk which has your laptop on it. The laptop is open again somehow, and he moves the mouse around the screen a bit to get rid of the screensaver. The house comes into view. Burnt and charred, bits of wood and plaster hanging from the singed remains. Snow covers the blackened floor, and piles up on the walls and what's left of the furniture. The contrast is beautiful, you think. Beautiful and sad. Just like death.

It's a sad thing, death, but you've got to stop and appreciate the beauty of it.

Your Grandmother's words that have stayed in the back of your head for the last twenty years echo through your mind once again. You see it all - a young version of yourself staring out at the frozen garden and all the dying plants. You shake your head to clear it, but you know that doesn't work. It never has. Those words started this whole business, and they'll never fade.

"It's all gone," Noah says, his voice barely a whisper. "It's really gone, isn't it."

"I'm afraid it is." For a moment you find yourself feeling sorry for the boy, but you tell yourself you're just tired and take another sip of your coffee.

The doorbell rings then. Noah jumps and looks at you with wide eyes. You put a finger to your lips and walk as naturally as you can towards the door. Shutting the inside door behind you, you open the outer one.

"Yes?"

An old lady stands staring at you, hands on her hips. You recognise her as somebody who lives in the apartment, but only from having seen her once or twice.

"It's a bit late to be having guests, isn't it?"

"Yes," you agree, trying to appear like you're not sure what her point is. "Why, do you want to come in?"

"You know what I mean. Who are you shouting with? I've been woken up by you making an awful lot of noise up here."

"I'm afraid I don't know what you mean, Ma'am." You put on your best 'polite and friendly voice'. "Maybe it was somebody different."

"No, I recognise your voice. Who have you got in there? I didn't know you had children."

"I don't."

"I heard a child. I only know too well the sound of an upset child shouting."

"Well, maybe I did hear something, but I was asleep so I don't know for sure. Perhaps you should check with the other neighbours?"

"I—"

You shut the door in her face before she can say anything else.

"What was that all about?" the boy asks as you shut the second door behind you.

"Nothing. You just need to be quieter." You add the recent event to your list of reasons to move and get your own place.

"I wouldn't have had to be quiet at all if you hadn't burned my house down," he mutters. "I wouldn't even have to be here."

You sigh for what feels like the thousandth time since you found him.

"How many times have you done it?" he asks suddenly.

"Done what?"

"Burnt somebody's house. This can't be the first time."

"I do it a lot," you say truthfully. It's not like he'll be able to tell anybody after tonight anyway. "I put cameras around the house and on another house so I can have a full view. Then I set the house on fire and watch it burn."

"And listen to the screams of innocent people dying at your hand."

"Well- yes. But that's not why I do it."

"Then why *do* you do it?"

"I . . ." You realise you've never really thought about it. "I don't actually know. I guess I've always liked fire, and I was so angry at what happened to my family that after living with my Grandmother for three years I decided at age sixteen that I'd had enough. And I set fire to a random house."

"And you carried on."

"I found I quite liked doing it. It was satisfying, to be the cause of something so beautiful."

"What, somebody else's death?"

"It's a sad thing, death," you say, quoting your Grandmother. "But you've got to stop and appreciate the beauty of it."

"That's sick. Everything about you is."

You shrug.

Noah stands up suddenly and looks around.

"Oh my god," he says. "I'm sitting in a room, on my own with a psychopath."

He runs towards the door and pulls on the handle. It doesn't move.

"It's locked," you say calmly. "You're not going anywhere.

Noah looks panicked and starts hitting the door.

"That's not going to work."

He starts shouting. "Help, somebody help!"

"Stop making a scene," you say, standing up and moving slowly towards him. He continues banging his fists on the door and shouting.

"Help!"

"Be quiet!"

You realise that unless you do something somebody is going to come and complain. Thinking quickly, you wrench open a drawer and pull out the first thing you see. Noah sees you and starts shouting louder, his voice cracking as tears slide down his face. Before he can do anything a tranquilliser dart is sticking out of his neck and he falls to the floor. You put the gun down and crouch next to him, putting a finger by his neck. He still has a regular pulse; he's just sleeping. You pull him up over your shoulder, cursing your lack of muscles as you lay him down on the bed.

Your words from earlier come back to you. *You're not special, kid. You survived by accident.*

Maybe you were wrong. Maybe there is something about him. How else could he have survived the inferno that killed his parents? You remember his eyes, when they stared deep into yours, angry or sad, or challenging you to say something. Every time, no matter what he was trying to say with them, they always looked sort of . . . *odd*. They almost shone, all the time.

You have an idea, and go back to search through the drawer where you keep the gun. Pushing other weapons aside, you find it. The syringe. You take it over to the sleeping boy and, peeling back his eyelid with one of your hands, you jab the needle into his forearm. Thick red blood starts to fill it as you pull it back. Once it's full Noah's eyes go dull. You look at the blood which shimmers in the light. Just like his eyes did.

Sirens start wailing in the distance. You have to get out of here. Looking back at his eyes to convince yourself, you take the blood and put it in an airtight bottle, which in turn you put in your pocket. You reach under the bed and take out a suitcase, full of the only things that matter to you. Everything else can stay here, including the boy.

You grab everything from the weapon drawer quickly and shove them into your suitcase. Fumbling with the keys in your haste, you manage to unlock the doors and dash down the stairs as quietly as you can. You run down to the basement and, standing in the safety of the door you take something out of your bag and throw it into the middle of the room.

You don't have much time now. The sirens are getting louder and the thing in the basement could go off any minute. You make your way out to your car, which is still waiting for you in the driveway. As quickly as you can you get in the car and jam the key in the ignition. It takes a while to start, but the engine sputters into life on the third try. You push your foot down on the pedal and the car speeds out onto the road. You're out of the way just in time as the building erupts into flames behind you.

You put a hand on the bottle in your pocket and smile to yourself. You've done it again. The boy is dead and you have his blood. The sirens get quieter as you drive in the opposite direction. You've done it.

You've escaped once again.

Fairytale of York

May
Her window is open, and I can hear the music again. It floats out into the air, drifting through my window as if it knows exactly where to go. It's always the same song, although I don't know what it's called. Something about Christmas, which is odd since it's April. I've been listening to her song every day for a week, since the moving vans came. Since then she's had her window open every day as she plays the song.

Caz
I turn the volume up on my iPod, trying to drown out any thoughts my brain dares to form. It's Easter, the time my thoughts run wild. I hate it, all of it, the memories, the two weeks where everyone's off school, even the chocolate eggs. *Another three days*, I tell myself. Three days then I'll be starting fresh, in a new school. No memories, nobody who knows my past.

May
I lean forward on my chair and rest my head on the windowsill. This is how I've spent the past week, listening to the music and trying to imagine what she's doing. I've seen her once outside the house, when she came. I was here and the vans arrived. She pulled up in a 4x4 a couple of minutes later and got out, blonde hair flying everywhere in the wind as she ran to the front door and disappeared.

Caz
Mum's told me I should leave the house, make the most of the nice weather since we don't get it very often in England. I tell her I will, but I never do. I can't bring myself to do it. Going to school will be hard enough, since I haven't been on a bus for a year.

May
I imagine she's dancing. I try to conjure up an image of her, but having only seen the back of her head for all of four seconds it isn't easy. The song reaches the end, and the only bit where I can properly understand the lyrics - *the bells are ringing out for Christmas Day*. The singers seem to be having an argument. It's a man and a woman, a cliché love story. They start out loving each other, then they fight and everything goes pear-shaped.

Caz
I go to press repeat on the song immediately. It was his favourite song, so I've played it countless times since. It's the only thing that reminds me of him in a good way, the only thing that doesn't have me in tears, completely broken. I don't know how I'll cope in school; I've been off for so long. *It's for the best*. And it will be. I'll be fine. A fresh start is all I need.

May
The song stops, but it doesn't start again. That's odd. Normally she presses repeat straight away. Maybe she's going to do something, I think, and decide that maybe I should too. I have three days left before I have to go back to school, and I want to make the most of it, even though

sitting here listening to her song is a perfectly good way to spend my days.

Caz

I change my mind and don't bother setting the song to go again. In fact I've had enough of listening to people who don't even exist argue through song. I lie on my bed, listening to the birds' song instead. They sound so happy, so free. Sometimes I wish I could just grow wings and fly away from everything, forever.

May

Somehow I end up lying on the floor, thinking of Christmas and love and things I don't even understand. I wonder if I'll ever see her, through my window or face to face. Although when I think about it, face to face probably won't go very well, I'd most likely end up crumpling or running away or saying something stupid.

Caz

The next three days pass too quickly. Before I know it I'm stumbling down the stairs at six in the morning trying to convince myself that there's nothing to worry about and the bus is safe. "You're sure you'll be okay?" my parents ask as I'm trying to leave. All I can do is nod. I don't trust myself to speak without blurting something out.

May

I sit in my usual seat on the bus. It's at the front, since all the other kids sit at the back where they can make as much noise as they want. The bus is about to pull out when there's a shout, "wait!" and somebody's running.

Caz

I just make it to the bus on time and thank the driver for waiting. I clamber up the steps and am greeted by so many faces, some confused, some genuinely interested. Most of them don't pay me any attention so that's good.

May
Somebody gets on the bus, and it's *her*, the girl who lives opposite me, the one who plays the music on full volume every day. I've never seen her face before, and I'm studying her when she turns and smiles at me. I make an attempt at a smile before turning my attention hurriedly back to my feet.

Caz
I settle down in a seat near the front. The other kids go back to shouting in the back like nothing happened, so I take out a book and start to read about people having a much better time than me. It helps to take my mind off my worries.

May
I see her a few times during the day. She's in quite a few of my classes, and I've learnt by now that her name is Caz. By the end of the day I still haven't managed to talk to her, so I tell myself I will tomorrow. It's unlikely, but then again, miracles can happen. Maybe my miracle will be finally finding some courage.

Caz
When I get back from school I ignore all Mum's questions and go straight out into the shed in the back garden. I pull out dusty old items I never knew we still had, and finally find it. Kayden's guitar. He played really well, and even taught me a bit once, although I haven't touched a guitar for years. I take it up to my room with me, and attempt to start playing.

May
When I open my window after school I realise the song isn't playing for once. Instead I hear faint guitar music, almost as if she's trying to play it. She's working out chords - finding all the notes and playing, before moving on to the next. A few times she gets frustrated, and I can see this taking a long time.

Caz
After the fourth time I get the same chord wrong, I put the guitar down on my bed to avoid throwing it across the room.

I decide I'll give up and turn the real song back on. I'll try again tomorrow.

May

On the third day the chords are coming along well, and after a while she starts singing along. *It was Christmas Eve, babe . . .* Her voice is beautiful; it floats out along the air like she has no idea I'm even listening. I start mouthing the words along with her, because by now I've learnt some of them.

Caz

I completely lose myself in the song, memories flooding my brain. Good ones, though. Kayden first showing me the song, us dancing to it together, Kayden playing his guitar. I tell myself I'm going to stop being miserable about it. Even though I'm still upset, I'm not going to let it affect my education. Tomorrow, I will make a friend.

May

I'm sat in my usual seat on the bus when Caz comes to sit by me. She looks just as shocked as I feel, almost like she can't quite believe she actually did what she just did. "I'm Caz," she says, introducing herself, and I tell her my name is May.

Caz

There's an awkward silence then as both of us wonder what to say next, then May says "you sing really well."

May

"Oh," she says. She sounds surprised, like she doesn't realise that people can hear when her window is open. "How . . . how do you know?"

Caz

My first worry is that she's been listening. Then I wonder how. Is she stalking me? Does she follow me everywhere without me knowing?

May

"You opened your window last night," I explain. "I live in the house opposite yours, so I can hear it. I've been listening since you moved, when you started playing the song."

Caz

"Oh," I say again, not quite sure how to react.

May

"What song is it?"

Caz

"It's called Fairytale of New York."

May

"Isn't it a Christmas song?"

Caz

I sigh. Everybody asks this same question when they hear me listening to it. "It's supposed to be. But it only mentions Christmas because that's when the lovers fell out. Other than that it isn't really that Christmassy. I don't think things that have just a little to do with Christmas should be banned the rest of the year."

May

"I guess so."

Caz

"I like the song anyway. It isn't fair that I shouldn't be able to listen to my favourite song just because it's a Christmas song."

May

She flicks her blonde hair over her face and opens a book, making me think I may have upset her. I ought to say something - I know I should, but I don't know what, and even if I knew exactly the words I'd never have the confidence to say them.

Caz

I try to act normal as I'm reading, but inside I'm panicking. The bus is picking up speed, and I can't help thinking about him. My face is hidden behind my hair, thank goodness, so May won't say anything. Hopefully.

May

The bus goes over a sudden bump and Caz draws a sharp breath, grabbing her seat with one hand, and my arm with the other.

Caz

"Sorry!" I say quickly, my voice coming out high and squeaky. I pull my hand off her and try to focus on my book again, even though my brain is everywhere but the page.

May

"A-are you okay?" I ask tentatively.

Caz

"Yeah, yeah. Fine." I'm aware that I'm speaking too quickly but there's not much I can do about it.

May

I don't push her again. It feels like everything I'm saying just irritates her even more. I tell myself I should just shut up for the rest of the journey.

Caz

Part of me thinks I should apologise, but then again there's always the possibility that if I do say something May will ask more, and I don't want to tell her anything. Not yet anyway.

May

Throughout the day Caz seems a bit off, until our last lesson of the day, when she passes me a small piece of folded up yellow paper as the bell rings for the end of the day. I unfold it hesitantly, not sure what to expect, but written on it is a mobile number in Caz's curly writing. I turn back to her, not sure what to say, but she's gone, disappeared into the crowd of teenagers eager to get home for the weekend.

Caz

I'm sat on my bed at home, Fairytale of New York playing on my iPod, when May texts. Nothing special, just *Hey, it's May*, but I text back excitedly.

May

The reply comes almost straight away. *Ha that rhymed :) Call me? The keyboard on my phone is rubbish.* I'm hesitant at first, but my thumb decides it's in charge and presses the ring button. I don't argue with it, and hold the phone to my ear instead.

Caz

"Hey," I say as soon as it's connected.

May

"Hey." Awkward silence.

Caz

I laugh nervously. "You can probably hear the music in the background."

May

I stop to listen, and find I can hear it. "Yeah. You're kinda predictable though, so even if I couldn't hear then I would've been able to guess what song it was."

Caz

"Yeah." I sigh.

May

"Hey, can I ask something? How come you love that song so much?"

Caz

"It's a good song." I shrug even though she can't see me.

May

"I guess, but you listen to it all the time."

Caz
"It . . . it was my brother's favourite song."

May
"Was?"

Caz
"Yeah. There was an accident last year, and . . ."

May
"Oh. Sorry."

Caz
I take a deep breath. "No, it's okay. I'm trying to deal with the grief, and telling people is a good way to get over something, right?"

May
"I guess so." I look around, searching for anything to change the subject. "Hey, you know what I think?"

Caz
I roll over on my bed. "What do you think?" I ask, half expecting some long lecture on family and grief and 'it'll all be okay' like I've had from all my family members every time I've seen them.

May
"Maths books should be yellow."

Caz
I burst out laughing, I can't help myself. That was definitely not what I was expecting. "And why is that?"

May
"Well, Maths is a yellow word, and, I don't know. It would just make more sense than the red ones we have."

Caz
"The word Maths is yellow?" I say between chuckles.

May
"Yeah . . . don't you have colours for words?"

Caz
"Um, no I don't think so."

May
Caz starts laughing, and I join in, and it becomes apparent then that I really like Caz. That would explain why I was so particularly shy to talk to her, and why I still panic every time I think I've said something wrong. At that point I make some hasty excuse about homework I ought to do in my red book and hang up.

Caz
I smile to myself as she ends the call. May's funny, and I hadn't realised. I don't even think she realises sometimes. Making a friend was obviously a good idea. I decide I need to start being more sociable, since it seems to be okay.

May
I stay in my room the rest of the night, listening to Caz singing through her window, and trying to work out the lyrics I don't know yet. The story won't make complete sense until I know all the words. Sometimes that's what my life feels like. I don't hear all the words clearly, so some things just don't make much sense. It's easier to ignore in life though, especially since I'll only ever hear it once. That song is on repeat every night.

Caz
I sit by May on the bus again on Monday. And Tuesday. We talk a lot during the week, and on Thursday, I ask if she wants to come home with me for the night. As soon as she's called her Mum and got approval, we sit on the bus and chatter endlessly. The awkward silences don't exist between us any more.

May
"What's the story of that song?" I ask, when Caz starts it playing quietly in the background. We're sat on the covered

wooden veranda in her back garden, watching the bugs fly around, lit up by the setting sun.

Caz
"It's sorta dark. It's about two Irish people who fall in love, and the man wins a lot of money betting on horses so he takes the two of them to New York. They hope to get big there, like all teens who move there do. They have big dreams and their love blocks out any bad possibilities for them."

May
"Sounds great."

Caz
"It is, until they realise that making life in New York is hard, and that it isn't all as good as it was made out to be. They start doing drugs, because they're young and unemployed and have nothing better to do. When they're high they fall out and in a rage, the woman goes and sleeps with another man. She feels guilty, abuses more, and ends up in a hospital barely alive because of her addiction."

May
"Oh, not so good then."

Caz
"Yeah. The man finds out about her cheating and they argue a lot and while she's in hospital he becomes really depressed and turns to drink. In the end he ends up in the drunk tank, which is a place like a prison cell for seriously drunk and dangerous people to stay until they've sobered up."

May
"Do they get back together?"

Caz
"It doesn't seem so."

May

"Oh." In that moment I'm glad that my love life, however non-existent, is better than that at least. "I've always wanted to go to New York," I say after a while.

Caz

I hesitate before speaking. "Well, I can't take you there, but we can always go to the original."

May

"The original?"

Caz

"Yeah. It's only a couple of hours drive up to York."

May

I laugh. "The original, eh? Aren't they pretty different?"

Caz

"Not if we pretend they aren't."

May

"And how are you going to get us there?"

Caz

"I've had my licence for a few weeks," I admit.

May

"Really? How?"

Caz

"The driving instructor thinks I'm seventeen, and technically it's only another five months until I am."

May

"But it's illegal."

Caz

"Not if my licence says I was born a year before I actually was. Besides, you can get a licence at 14 in parts of the US."

May
I grin despite myself. "I can't believe you."

Caz
"So what d'you say? Shall we run away to York?"

May
I pause for a bit to consider. Then I think, *why not?* "Sure!" I say, grinning like I never have before.

Caz
After school the next day, we run home from the bus stop and agree to meet by my house in half an hour. I've been waiting in the car for a while and am about to ring her when May shows up.

May
"Sorry I'm so late," I say, clambering in on the passenger side. "My parents took a while to convince. After a bit I told them that I'm sixteen and it's technically legal for me to move out now, so they should be glad I'm only gone for the weekend."

Caz
"You told them?"

May
"Yeah . . . Didn't you?"

Caz
"No. I just left a little note saying I was taking the car and I'd be back sometime on Sunday. It's easier to ask forgiveness than to get permission after all."

May
"I got permission."

Caz
"Yeah, well. Your parents are obviously nicer than mine. They'd never let me go after what happened with Kayden."

May
"Who?"

Caz
"My brother."

May
"Oh."

Caz
I clear my throat. "Anyway. Let's go, time's a-wasting!"

May
She hits her foot down on the pedal and for a minute I panic. Then I remember she's had lessons, so although she's too young she knows what she's doing. "We're actually doing this," I say, to break the silence.

Caz
"Yeah we are. You nervous?"

May
"No," I say, because I'm actually not. I giggle, my new-found confidence making me dizzy.

Caz
"Although you gotta promise me one thing."

May
"What?"

Caz
"We won't fall out and do drugs."

May
"Never."

Caz
I wind down the window and turn the radio up, playing something other than Fairytale of New York for once, and we laugh as we join the main road, pretending we're going on a big adventure rather than a little hotel in York.

May
We pull up at the hotel Caz has booked just over two hours later. It's nothing special, just a little room with a sofa, coffee table and two beds. And a window. The window is the best bit. It overlooks the lake the hotel is built by, and the sun is low in the sky causing specks of light to dance across the water's surface. A gentle hill sits on the opposite side of the lake, the sun making the rock shine a sort of golden colour.

Caz
We rent a pedalo and take it out on the lake. A little way out May gets her phone out and starts Fairytale of New York playing. I start singing along to the words and before long she joins in.

May
I trail my hand in the water as we pedal across the lake, the music filling the air. I look over at Caz, her hair blowing out behind her, a big smile on her face. She's completely lost in the music, she doesn't seem to care who might be listening to her sing at this point. We reach the end and belt out the last words. "*The boys of the NYPD choir still singing 'Galway Bay'. And the bells are ringing out for Christmas Day.*"

Caz
"Did you know there isn't actually an NYPD choir?" I ask as the song stops.

May
"Is there not?"

Caz
"No. NYPD stands for New York Police Department, so it's probably an ironic reference to the boys in the drunk tank singing. It's supposed to show that it isn't such a great place

after all since there isn't a choir, instead a bunch of drunk lads who've been put in a sort of prison."

May
"Oh right. That's cool." We reach the other side of the lake and pull the boat up onto the shore so that it doesn't float away, then head down a little path leading through the reeds. It's looking pretty uninteresting and we're about to turn around when we follow the path around a corner.

Caz
We stop to take in the view for a second. The reeds come to an end suddenly and the ground is covered in the greenest grass. We seem to have come in a sort of semicircle, so now we're back at the lake, the setting sun sending orange sparks bouncing over the ripples. The hill behind us comes down in an almost vertical drop, a smooth sheet of rock entering the water. At the bottom is a little wooden bench, and it's here that we settle ourselves.

May
"This is our own story," I say, holding my arms out to the lake. "The Fairytale of York."

Caz
"Yeah. You've just gotta pretend we're somewhere more romantic."

May
I turn and stare at her. Did I hear her right? I'd thought it was just me. I fumble for the right words, but all I end up saying is "why?"

Caz
"Well- wouldn't you like it to be?" I worry now that I shouldn't have said anything, but I just didn't see the point in keeping quiet any more. I've dropped enough hints, and I can't blame May for not picking up on them. I didn't make them that obvious anyway. I gave up, and now I've said it.

May
"But this is perfect."

Caz
She looks at me then, and I look back at her. It's that look that shatters my doubt, sending it flying far away, and as I lean towards her, I don't worry about whether it's the right time or if she wants it too, because I know it's right. She said so herself, it's perfect.

May
The kiss is everything I'd ever hoped it would be, and more. It sends shivers up my spine, and I think about how when I was small and would have been disgusted by the idea of kissing anyone outside my family. Five years ago I would never have done something like this; now I don't want it to end.

Caz
Neither of us says anything when we finally pull away, we just sit there watching the sun set. When it's completely dark we don't discuss going back to the boat, we just do. As we pedal out onto the lake neither of us says we're going to stop in the middle, and yet we do. Neither of us says anything until it's pitch black and the moon is out and we wrap our arms around each other to keep warm.

May
"It's my month," I whisper. Because it is. It's four minutes past midnight on Saturday the first of May.

Caz
"Were you born in May?"

May
"No, oddly enough. My birthday is the third of February. I guess my parents just liked the name."

Caz
"I like the name."

May
"When's your birthday?"

Caz
"September the fifteenth, but I don't celebrate it."

May
"Why not?"

Caz
"I just think it's another ordinary day. Nobody gives you presents when it's three years since you started school, so why when it's three years since you started life? It's just stupid, people giving you presents because you survived another year, like they don't think you'll make it. Since what happened with Kayden I told my family I didn't want to get gifts on my birthday, because it felt too much like they had been expecting me to die too and were celebrating when I didn't."

May
I'm not sure what to say, she sounds so bitter. I wonder whether I shouldn't have said anything, but then how was I going to know she'd get upset? I start to wonder whether this is going to work, I'm always so scared I'll say something wrong around her. Before I can say anything Caz speaks again.

Caz
"We were on a bus when it happened."

May
"When what happened?"

Caz
"The bus went over a bump and the driver had a fit. The bus swerved onto the pavement and smashed into a shop. Kayden and I were in the front on the side which hit the shop, him by the window. He took all the force, and I survived."

May

"That's why you got scared when the school bus went over a bump. When you grabbed my arm."

Caz

"Yeah. I didn't want to tell you anything but I don't think we should be keeping anything big from each other any more. And like I said, telling people helps you deal with the grief."

May

"I guess it does." I start pedalling gently and Caz joins in.

Caz

"Sorry," I whisper as we reach the shore. May nods, letting me know it's all okay, and we go silently up to our room. We collapse onto the beds and May is asleep before I can even try to start a conversation. I smile to myself and tuck her in like a little child, then take myself off to bed.

May

I'm woken in the morning by the sun prising my eyelids open. I sit up in bed and read for a bit, until Caz wakes up and we get dressed. I watch her brush her golden hair and wonder whether last night was all a dream. She seems so perfect, too good to be true.

Caz

"Can I plait your hair?" May asks. I nod, handing her my brush and we sit in front of the mirror as her fingers work their way through my hair, pulling it up into a French plait that hangs down my back.

May

When I'm done, we head out and go explore the area. Caz googles and finds an adventure park nearby, and although I'm reluctant at first we go to check it out. She takes me on rollercoasters and rides so fast, round and round until I feel sick and can't stand up straight. We fall into each other, laughing despite the dizziness.

Caz
"Oh my gosh, we've *got* to go on that," I say once we've recovered. May follows my gaze and sees that I'm pointing to the big wheel. Except this isn't just a big wheel. It's huge, bigger than any one I've ever seen before. The words 'Mega Wheel' are spelled out on the side in flashing lights.

May
"Sure," I say, relieved it isn't another thrill ride. We queue up for what feels like ages but is only really about three minutes. Caz grabs my arm and practically drags me into a carriage, as if she's afraid I won't want to go on. I want to tell her I love these things, but I don't say anything.

Caz
We're almost at the top when the wheel comes to a halt. There's a loud clicking noise and the carriage swings slightly.

May
"What was that?"

Caz
"Relax, it happens sometimes."

May
Caz puts her arm around my shoulder and I shudder in the good way I've only felt once before. She keeps it there as the wheel starts again and we stand up to admire the view. When the carriage comes to a stop at the bottom she opens the door and curtsies, holding out her hand to help me out.

Caz
"Your majesty," I say as she takes my hand, giggling. I spin her around and we end up with arms around each other, and I lean down and kiss her, trying to remember how I did it last night. Music is playing somewhere in the background, and I rock her in time to it.

May
Now I'm certain it wasn't a dream. Otherwise we wouldn't be here, her hands weaving into my hair, her lips on mine. It's

real, and it's happening to me. My own story - not like the ones I've read, and definitely not like Caz's song.

Caz
We agree the next morning to leave pretty early. The note I left my parents isn't the most detailed, and they're probably getting mad that I haven't been answering my phone. We check out of the hotel and thanks to the lack of traffic we're back in less than two hours. I drop May off at her house and then pull the car into the drive. She gives me a thumbs-up to say *good luck* before disappearing into the house. I brace myself for the scolding I'm about to get.

May
I don't hear from Caz for the rest of the day. I tell myself it makes sense; she ran away without telling her parents where she was, so most likely she doesn't have her phone or anything. I can't help but worry, though.

Caz
I see May in school the next day and we smile at each other from opposite sides of the class. I slip her a little note during a Maths lesson to tell her that I've been banned from all technology for two days, and grounded for a week, but it was worth it. She laughs and says it's okay and that's that.

May
A couple of days later I'm in my room doing homework when my phone buzzes. A text from Caz. *You were handsome, you were pretty. Queen of New York City.* I grin, she's quoting Fairytale of New York. Or maybe she means it . . .

Caz
When the reply doesn't come, I text her the next line. *When the band finished playing we howled out for more.* That one doesn't have as much significance but I send it anyway.

May
I move my chair over to the window as I text back. By now I've learnt all the lyrics off by heart, so I send Caz the next line. *Sinatra was swinging, all the drunks they were singing.* I

start humming the tune softly as I wait for her to reply. I stop as I realise what the next line is.

Caz

I smirk as I type the line she's left me with. I look up through my window, and there she is, her eyes reflecting the setting sun, her dimple just showing as she tries not to smile. I mouth 'I love you' as I send the message. *We kissed on the corner and danced through the night.*

May

I smile at her because that's what we did. And even though the rest of the song is nothing like anything I'd ever consider doing, those four lines couldn't be more accurate.

Caz

She grins, rests her head on the windowsill and mouths the four special words. *I love you too.*

The Top

This is how it ends. With your head held high and your dignity still intact.

And as the guards lead you from your cell, you walk with them confidently, as though you can't hear your wife's last screams getting quieter and quieter as you leave her behind, as though you can't already hear the jeers and insults that will be thrown at you.

As though you don't know it's the end.

That's how you'd planned to leave. You'd let them know that you don't regret anything, you'd let them know you aren't afraid. Because you're not. No matter how much you tell yourself you should be, you aren't. Despite all your efforts, you can't convince yourself that you're scared. Not of anything. Maybe you just knew this day was coming.

The guards turn an unexpected corner. You look around you, confused. This isn't the way you were supposed to go, you're certain of it. You've memorised the way so that you'd know when your time had come. So that when they came, you'd have some warning.

This is the second thing that's gone differently to how you had it planned. The first was when they actually told you where they were taking you. You'd watched it happen to so many others. The guards would come, they'd mumble something about going somewhere with them then they'd take hold of an arm each and never return. You knew all along where they were going, every time. You'd heard the guards' conversations and worked out exactly when each of you would go.

Today was your day. So when the guards walked in and told you they were moving you to a different cell, you couldn't help but be a little surprised. As they started walking along the corridor, with you in between them, you considered the fact that it was a trick. Everything else had been exactly how it should, so maybe they just said that so that you wouldn't panic. You wanted to tell them that you were far from panicking, then they turned the corner.

Now you're almost certain it isn't a trick. They're taking you the wrong way; it must be something else. As they turn yet another corner and lead you up a spiral staircase you begin to think something is very wrong. You didn't even know this place existed until now.

You reach the top of the staircase, and a few feet in front of you is a door. One of the guards opens the door and the other shoves you into the room behind it. Before you can even say anything the door is shut, and the only goodbye you get is the jangling of keys and the click of the lock.

It definitely wasn't a trick. They really have moved you to another cell, only this one doesn't have a window and there are no neighbours. In your old cell you could talk to the others through the bars, although you didn't always feel like talking. Most of your conversations with them were made up of complaints about the food, the guards, anything anyone could think of, so long as it was negative. There were some days when you could just do without all that, days when all you wanted to do was get up and shout *we're all here, we all know how bad it is, so shut your bloody mouth!* You've lost count of how many times that sentence has gone through your mind.

Other days it did you more good. On those days you started off with a rant about something or other, and ended up on the floor clutching your sides. Some of the other inmates could be really funny.

You like to call them inmates. Not prisoners, it sounds too much like they've done something wrong. Of course, there would be people who'd say that what they did was wrong, but you think it was right, which is why you tried too. There are others, still in the outside world who think it was right too, they just didn't have the confidence to do anything. That makes you feel braver, like you maybe did some good despite the fact it landed you in jail.

Except you can't really call it jail. It's different to the ones you'd read about. You knew right from the start when the guards dragged you in with nothing but a dark grey uniform and a wristband bearing the letters *D.S.*. They walked you past people with different bands, ones with numbers on instead, then threw you carelessly in a cell and left. It was a while before you learnt from the other inmates that the numbers were how long each prisoner had to stay here.

D.S. stood for *Death Sentence*.

You wonder now why you're here instead of crouched with your head on the block waiting for the blade to fall. What is the point of this small stone cell, and how is it different to your old one?

•••

A few minutes after you start to wonder when lunch will be, a small hatch opens in the wall and a plate of food slides out. Your first thought is *really?* then you realise what this means.

You'll have to have your meals here, in this cell. No going down to dinner with the other inmates, no socialising. As much as you hate it you find yourself craving the noisy, cramped hall in which you used to have all your meals.

This is their plan. They're going to leave you here completely on your own. That's why there's no window, no neighbours, no mealtimes with everybody else, just a stupid little hatch in the wall through which your food is pushed. No human contact at all.

"Hey!" you shout through the wall. No reply. "Hey, assholes! Very crafty, but isn't this just wasting time?"

After a few moments a hoarse voice whispers back to you.

"We're not wasting time, we have all the time in the world, unlike you." Laughter echoes through the wall which gets quieter as the person owning the voice moves further away.

"Wait, what? Why am I here?" The voice doesn't reply and you start kicking the wall and shouting louder. "*Why am I here?*"

You stop as you realise that this is what you're supposed to do. That's why you're here; they're going to leave you until you go insane, then they'll take you for the chop. You'd always sort of looked forward to the day when it would happen, because it would all be over. There was no point looking forward to anything else because you were sentenced to be here for the rest of your life, not that it would be very long. You'd always thought that it would be quick and reasonably painless, so you'd had that to look forward to.

What now? Your wristband still tells you you're supposed to die, so why haven't you? You pull at it in frustration, the two letters mocking you. You can almost hear them laugh, that's what this room is doing to you. You tug at them in vain until your fingers are sore and you collapse on the small, hard bed in the corner.

You're woken the next morning by the sound of the metal hatch opening again. Your breakfast slides in and sits on the floor, tempting you over with its smell.

"You're having a laugh," you mutter. They can't really expect you to stay here, can they? You haven't really done anything wrong, surely they'll let you out sooner or later.

By the end of the day you're pretty certain they won't. You've spent a whole day in here with nothing to do but sit on the cold stone floor and stare at the cold stone wall. Your mind keeps going back to that dreadful day, and try as you might you cannot think of anything you did to deserve your sentence. Fair enough, some of what you did was wrong, but you'd seen others who did worse, and it was all in a good cause. Sort of.

You remember the day like it was yesterday and not six months ago. He stood in the square, perched on a plastic box because the little bastard wanted to be heard properly. He'd hung a wooden cross on the fountain behind him to attract attention. Nobody gave him any at the start, but then a small group stopped to listen for a while. Soon enough, people started gathering round, at first just to see what was going on, but since they stuck about they must have agreed with the preacher.

At one point a few of them started nodding to each other, and that's when you began to see the angry faces gathering around you, their expressions mirroring yours. This preacher knew nothing, who was he to talk about matters like this? Damn these Catholics and their funny ideas about things.

The crowd cheered and someone ran into their midst. The others followed; so did you. There were shouts and cries, letting loose all the anger you'd had locked up inside you since the start. This preacher was just one of many, although he seemed to be the craziest. You'd teach him and all his followers.

You didn't realise how many Jews lived in your town until that day. There were loads of you, all screaming, outraged at what the snobby little Catholic man thought he could say about them. His cross was knocked to the floor and smashed into little pieces. Someone was cheering and suddenly you all were, and then you lost control of your actions, caught up in the excitement of rebelling against the people who'd discriminated you for such a long time. Separate bathrooms, separate restaurants, shops you weren't allowed to go into because of your religion. It was stupid, but nobody had ever had the courage to stand up to it.

Until then. There were so many of you it was impossible to be afraid of anything. You remember looking at your wife through the crowd and grinning, and she grinned back because of the relief, then her expression faded. Her face paled and she tried to mouth something to you. You didn't understand it at the time but you've kicked yourself so many times since about how you should have been able to work it out.

Watch out!

Except you didn't. You couldn't, that's what you keep reminding yourself. You didn't know what she was saying, so you couldn't have dodged the hand that came flying towards you, wrapping itself around your neck. You couldn't have avoided being dragged away, kicking and screaming, struggling for breath.

Most of you were caught. You remember overhearing a couple of the guards talking, one of them saying that a few of the 'scum' had got away. You remember being disgusted at the time, but after a while you got used to the comments. A couple of weeks in you learnt from another inmate that the ones who weren't sentenced to death were the Christians who joined in. They were arrested too for rebelling, but they weren't to be killed because they weren't Jewish. That was the worst crime anyone could commit around here.

You sigh to yourself as you remember the first meal in this place. The guards led you in a single file line to the big hall, and you were each allowed a plate with which you could go and collect two slices of pork. 'No more, no less' they said.

You were understandably outraged, as was everyone else, but there was nothing you could do. The guards had guns and bulletproof vests, and all you had was your uniform and that bloody wristband. So like everyone else, you picked up your two slices and, like everyone else, you forced yourself to eat them. Then you rushed back to your cell and when the guards weren't looking you made yourself throw up and prayed for forgiveness. You promised you'd never eaten anything bad before and you never would again.

You couldn't keep that promise, of course. The guards took it upon themselves to organise two days a week where they'd serve something they knew was against your law, as a punishment for breaking theirs.

On a good day you'd try and work out how many times you'd broken your rules by being force-fed banned meats, but today you just can't be bothered. Your mind is everywhere but the present, so caught up in worrying about the past and the future that you know you wouldn't be able to focus long enough to count to ten, let alone calculate how many unlawful meals you've had.

•••

By the fifth day you're beginning to lose the plot. You spend the day pacing, wondering how long they intend to keep you here. When the hatch opens and gives you your meal of unlawful food you pick up the plate and throw it at the wall. You wrench the hatch open so that whoever sent the food can hear you.

"You're taking the piss!" you scream.

You're about to slam the hatch shut again when you hear a distant but familiar voice from somewhere far below you.

"Who is that?"

You know that voice anywhere, even if she had the flu and could barely speak you'd know it was her. Your wife.

"That's none of your business," a voice you assume is the cook says.

"Why is he up there?" she asks again. "What are they doing to him?"

"Listen, Miss, you'd better sit down and be quiet right now or—"

There's a thud and for a moment you worry what he's done to her, then you hear her voice.

"No, you listen to me," she hisses. "You don't know what I'm capable of, but looking at you I doubt you have any hidden strength. So, I want you to tell me exactly why he's up there, and nobody will get hurt."

"I-I . . ."

"Tell me! Tell me exactly what's going on in this place!"

"I don't know why he's up there," the cook manages. "The guards only told me to give him his food."

"Are you sure? Because I can always go talk to the guards if you want."

"No, no! That's all they told me I swear!"

He sighs as she lets go of him, and you're about to close the hatch when he speaks again.

"But, I did overhear a couple of them talking."

"When? What did they say?"

"It was about a week ago. One of them was saying that they were going to take him for the chop, and the other said he had a better idea."

"What was it?" your wife asks, voicing your exact thoughts.

"He said your husband was too cocky, that being in a cell for six months hadn't done him enough harm. He said they should take him up to the Top for a week or so, teach him a lesson. Nobody would pay to see someone who wanted to be killed, they pay for fear."

"What's the Top?"

"A tower that nobody but the guards is supposed to know about. Right at the top is a single cell, no windows, one door. He'll be kept there in solitary confinement until he cracks, then they'll take him. A shivering mess draws more crowds than someone who stares the executioner directly in the eye until the last moment."

You stop listening then. You were right all along - the guards want you to lose it. They have fun seeing you suffer. That must be why they've strung the executions out so that they're still happening six months later. They enjoy it. They enjoy your pain.

You slam the hatch shut again and lean against the wall. You take a deep breath, hoping to calm yourself but instead just breathing in a whole load of meat smell, making you feel even worse. Your heartbeat quickens, the walls suddenly feeling like they're closing in. You realise for the first time how small the room really is. Or maybe it's got smaller. For all you know it has, and you don't even question it any more. Things that never seemed possible before could be possible now; you don't have the brain power to doubt anything.

You punch your fist into the wall, hoping to relieve your stress. Nothing happens, except that your knuckles go red. Still you find yourself doing it again, and again. After a while you stop feeling the pain and sink to the floor, your face salty with tears you didn't know you'd cried. The monotonous pounding of your fist against the wall still rings in your ears, or maybe it's your heart beating, or maybe somebody's trying to get in.

Or out.

You stand up and stagger over to the bed, and the room is leaning and you're leaning and somehow you're on the floor and you don't even care, the room spins and you spin and you close your eyes to stop the nausea and . . .

The clicking of a key in the lock wakes you the next morning. The sun would probably be shining through the window if you had one, but you don't know that you'd care if it was. You sit up as the guards come in. They take an arm each and haul you up, and you're aware of the pain in your back. Sleeping on the stone floor did you no good. You would make a note to yourself never to do it again, but the look in the guards' eyes tells you you probably won't have another night to spend, never mind where it is. This is it. They're taking you for the chop.

You look down at your hands, which are shaking as they lead you down the stairs. So much for not being afraid. Your knuckles are bruised and swollen, your fingernails cracked and bleeding. Your back aches, your legs tremble, and your mind screams at you for looking so weak. You reach the bottom of the stairs and the guards continue to take you the way you knew you were supposed to go. Only now you couldn't be more afraid.

Out through a door and you're greeted by the cheers of thousands of Catholics, all gathered here to watch you suffer. Your face is damp again as you're walked up to the block, and somebody's murmuring *no . . . no . . .* It takes you a moment to realise the person is you.

You crouch down and rest your head on the block, still murmuring, to yourself more than anyone else. The words have changed now, but you can't tell what they are. Not that you care anyway. There's a noise of scraping metal and the crowd cheers. If this had just happened when it was meant to you would have shouted something at them, but you have no control over any part of your body. The blade is raised. You wait for it to fall.

This is how it ends. With your head bent over the block, and your dignity left shattered over the cell floor.

Martha

I open the door to her room and let myself in. On the way, I switch her music off so that she'll listen to me, and sit myself down on the bed beside her.

"Hey," I say. "I've missed you."

She doesn't reply, just keeps staring at the curtains drawn tightly across her window.

"Maybe you should open those," I suggest. "Let some light in."

She still doesn't move so I get up and go over to the curtains myself. The blue fabric folds slightly under my fingers, and it feels so good to be touching them again. I pull them open and tuck them to the side with the ties, letting light flood the room.

"That might do you some good."

The light only makes her look even more pale and sick, emphasising the huge dark circles around her eyes. I want her to get out the house, to do something. I can't stand seeing her like this. She grabs her phone and turns the music back on, louder this time. It's hopeless, I decide. She won't listen to me.

I spot her chalkboard lying on the floor behind her bed. It's sat there for years; unused and unloved. I pull it out into the centre of the room and write with a chalk, *come outside with me*. I watch her face for a reaction as she reads it. Her eyes flit over the words a few times, as if she can't quite believe what she's reading. I sigh impatiently. I don't understand what she doesn't get about it. I'd drag her outside if I could, but those were the rules. Don't touch anyone, and don't look them in the eye.

"Come on," I insist.

It was probably also mentioned that nobody would be able to hear anything I said, but I can't help getting frustrated with her. Why she can't just get up and go is beyond me. I get up to turn her music off again and thrust the chalkboard in her face. A wave of relief washes over me as she finally reacts, but the movement in her hand is only to push the board away. She probably hoped it'd go clattering across the floor, but of course I'm still holding it so it stays suspended in mid-air.

"Who are you?"

With those three words it's like she's stabbed me. The pain is unbearable. I'd hoped she'd at least know who I was, but thinking about it now I have no reason to really believe that. But the way I'd marched into her room like I owned the place, the way I'd kept turning her music off - it was all things I'd have done *before*. Surely she'd have realised by now?

Clearly she hadn't. The chalkboard tumbles out of my hand in slow-motion, landing on the floor with an exaggerated crash.

Everything is too much; I need to get her to see. Without thinking, I grab her arm and pull her out of her room. I drag her downstairs, ignoring her struggles, and only let go when we reach the garden. I turn to face her, to see if she's figured anything out, but all her face shows is fear. Complete and utter terror that freezes her to the spot. I realise with a twinge of despair like I've never felt before that she has no idea who I am. I've been forgotten.

Then she surprises me. She squints in my direction, and she's actually *looking* at me. Her eyes widen and I can see the joy light up her face.

"Martha?" she whispers.

"Yes," I say, my voice echoing around me, sounding alive and healthy. *I have a voice*. "Yes, yes! It's me, Martha! Your sister!"

A huge grin has found its way onto her face, but she still doesn't move.

"Am I dreaming?" She reaches out to touch my face, and it feels amazing. I lean into her hand as her fingers stroke my hair, just like she used to do when we were both alive and young. I'm not jealous of her for surviving because I'm here. I'm here and I exist, and that's all I could want right now.

"I'm dreaming."

I suddenly register what she's said.

"No, no you're not. I really am here, I promise. I came back for you."

She smiles. "I know you would do that if you could."

"But I have, I'm here now. You're not dreaming."

She continues to smile, gazing lovingly into my eyes as she moves her hand down to my shoulder. My eyes aren't gazing lovingly back anymore. I push her hand off my shoulder.

"I'm not supposed to touch anyone," I say, angrily.

"Why not? Touching me seemed to bring you back to life." She laughs, but I don't see anything funny.

"I'm not supposed to look you in the eye either."

She sighs. "I'm so glad you're here."

I realise she's not listening to me anymore, not really. None of what I'm saying is properly going into her brain. She probably still thinks she's dreaming.

"*Please* listen to me," I say, getting slightly frustrated with her now. "I am really here; I promise you're not dreaming. I came back for you!"

She nods sleepily, and it's obvious she doesn't believe me.

I carry on anyway. "But I was told not to touch anyone or look them in the eye, so I don't know what will happen now that I've done both."

"I've missed you . . ." she mumbles.

"You're missing the point!"

Her eyes are glassy and unfocused, and her head is tilted to one side.

"Please stay," she says.

"What?"

"I don't want to go."

"You're not. Nobody is."

Her knees give way and she lands on the grass beneath us. She lifts her head slowly, as though that one movement takes more effort than she has the energy for. When she looks at me I can see the tears shining in her eyes, and her bottom lip shakes as she speaks.

"I only wanted you back."

"What d'you mean?"

"What have I done?"

The part of her sleeve where I grabbed her arm starts to smoke. If it hurts her, she doesn't show it. Before long her whole arm is just a smoky shape at the side of her body, and the rest of her is quick to follow. I grab at her outline, trying desperately to stop whatever's happening, even though I have no clue what I'm doing. My fingers catch on the edge of her hoodie, and by the time I've worked out what it is, her clothes are the only thing left of her. The only proof that I'd been having a conversation with my sister a little while before.

"No," I shout at nothing. "No! I'm sorry. I'm so, so sorry." I bury my face in her hoodie to try and muffle the screams that come involuntarily from my mouth. The fabric is warm and damp from all my tears. I'm back, but now she's gone. All I wanted was to see her again; I just wanted to make her happy once more. This pale, peaky child was not the sister I knew, and I wanted to convince her that my death wasn't all bad, that she needed to move on. I just wanted to make her happy, and now she's gone.

Her words from earlier ring in my ears: *I only wanted you back*. Had she thought about it before? Had her desperation to see me again somehow willed me to come back for her?

I shove my face in the fabric of her hoodie again and mumble, "What do you mean?" Nobody answers, only this time I'm not entirely sure I'm talking to her.

insomnia

i am afraid.

why do my hands shake? i wish they'd stay still. somebody's going to notice something soon.

i'm cold. i think i like the cold though. it's better than being hot. i don't think that's why i'm shaking.

perhaps i should close the window. actually, never mind. they're so filthy i wouldn't be able to see the stars, and i love the stars.

what is a car doing driving past at this time of night? has something happened? maybe somebody's back from a late night party or something. it's none of my business anyway.

it's so dark. i love the dark, and i love the cold. so what am i scared of?

the cobwebs look pretty in the moonlight. perhaps i should clean them while i have nothing to do. but they're so pretty so maybe i'll leave them. still nothing to do.

the spiders aren't in their webs. i wonder where they've gone. maybe they're off hunting flies. no, don't spiders just wait for the stupid buggers to come to them? that's slightly cruel, but it's effective, and i guess the flies should see it coming.

i'd love to be a spider. all i'd have to do is sit in my web all day and wait for food to come to me. i could just sleep until food made itself, eat, then sleep again. oh man how i'd love to sleep.

maybe i should read to pass the time. i don't think i have any good books in here actually; most of them are downstairs. shame. though i probably wouldn't be able to focus on reading anyway.

will people wake up if i play the guitar? probably. even if i play really quietly they'd probably hear, and if they didn't it still wouldn't be very enjoyable since i'd be working so hard to stay quiet. when i relax and play it's very loud.

i could take my guitar out with me. what would people think if they walked past and saw me playing my guitar in the middle of the night? they'd probably ask questions, and that's the last thing i need.

i can't play anyway. my hands are shaking.

i am afraid.

i love the dark. i love the cobwebs. i love the spiders. i love the silence. i love the peace.

i hate the fear.

why am i scared i wonder?

my nails are too long. i should cut them. it'll be something to do anyway. now, where are the clippers? ah. there we go. so now i'll—

crap. clearly this isn't something to do in the dark. i wonder if it's bleeding. it feels okay. i probably just cut some skin off. maybe i'll put the clippers back and wait until the morning.

i wish my bedside lamp was working. then i could do something. i just don't want to think. i need something to distract myself with.

huh, that's a cool cloud. oh who am i kidding, it's just the same as the rest. i suppose it's still cool, though. funny how they look dark and menacing at night when they've spent all day being fluffy and inviting. they've gone from something you'd want to sleep on to something you'd want to avoid.

i wonder if he's thinking about me.

no, stop. that's stupid, i shouldn't think about it.

but still, i'd love to know if he is thinking about me.

of course he isn't; he'll be asleep at this time.

well i don't know that for certain. he could be sitting on his bed awake, like me. maybe he doesn't ever sleep either. or maybe he's staying up to be a rebel, messaging some girl to show her he's cool.

why can't i be that girl?

if he is messaging anyone, i know exactly who it would be. i've seen him look at her in the corridors, the way he winks at her as he passes. he probably thinks i haven't noticed, but i have. i always notice.

does that mean i'm always watching him? i guess it does. is that weird?

she'll go to bed eventually, and then he'll be sat there with nobody to message. if he'd messaged me i would have been happy to talk to him all night. it's not like i have anything better to do.

would that be depriving him of sleep? would it be wrong? maybe it's best for him that he message her, since she'll have some sort of curfew. there's no way her parents would allow her to stay up every night. that might be better for him. maybe he needs somebody who has a bedtime.

oh that's just ridiculous. he doesn't worry about that sort of stuff. he doesn't care if his girl goes to bed at nine or three.

or never.

except he must, because he still chose her instead of me.

no, he chose her because she's pretty, and i'm not. he doesn't care when his girl goes to bed, all he cares about is three things:

she has curves;
she's not embarrassing to be seen with;
she'll sleep with him whenever he pleases.

oh and his girl can't care how he treats her. he doesn't want somebody who will get up and leave if he mistreats her. he needs a dumb chick with a good body and no brain, and that's all he cares about.

why do i still want to be his girl then? if he's such a dick then why can't i stop thinking about him? it's not even like he's good-looking or anything . . .

okay, i can't even kid myself, he is *hella* good-looking. but surely that can't be it. there must be some other reason i want him to notice me.

i need to stop thinking about him. it does nobody any good, and even if he notices me, i don't want to be treated like a piece of meat. i'm not a toy, and neither is whatever poor sex-hungry creature he's convinced to get under him this time. she probably had it coming, but still.

it's disgusting. he's disgusting. i need to stop fantasising about him.

he's not for me.

but still, he asked if i was okay earlier, so maybe that means he does have a heart under all the fake tan and muscles and swagger. maybe he is thinking about me.

actually, i hope he's not. ugh, that was embarrassing. for him to see me like that . . .

i can't stand it when people pity me. they act like it's not my fault, and it is most definitely my fault. everything is my fault.

i'm doing it again. i need to stop *thinking*.

oh where did the cobwebs go? maybe the light from the moon just moved, or perhaps the spiders are moving house. maybe there aren't enough flies here.

i'd love to live like that. a spider's life seems so easy. well, when they're not being crushed by dad's shoes or getting washed down the sink. that's probably why they all live up so high. survival of the fittest; those who are stupid enough to run across the floor get squished. although if they survive running across the floor then they're obviously smart enough to survive, so it works both ways.

do guys like him survive then because they're willing to get any girl pregnant? is he helping the species by shoving himself into girl after girl? maybe that's why the population is getting gradually more stupid. those with brains settle down with a family and have one or two kids, while people like him manage to produce ten offspring a year who'll all inevitably end up like him.

i'm thinking about him again. ugh i need to stop. if he's so bad then why is he always on my mind?

maybe it's him i'm scared of. there's definitely something. why does the thought of school tomorrow send chills down my spine? i'm not normally this scared.

my hands are still shaking.

i am afraid.

i hate feeling like this. i wish i could sleep.

focus on the stars. they're so pretty. they sparkle so brightly. i love the stars.

that's the biggest cliché ever. how people's eyes sparkle when you love them. people's eyes can't sparkle, not unless they're facing the sun, but then their eyes would melt and they'd be blind. not so pretty any more.

his eyes don't sparkle. i wonder if that means i don't like him. well, i obviously do. i can't help it. even though he's so disgusting i can't help loving him. still, his eyes have never sparkled.

maybe i could change him. maybe if i was his girl, i could make him less of the dick he makes himself out to be and more of the soft boy i saw earlier today. he definitely cares about others, so what's this reputation he's given himself?

actually, i don't want to be his girl now. not after what he saw today. i don't think i can talk to him. he might ask. i hate when people see me like that. the tears on my face, the bruises on my knuckles. they all look the same, whenever anyone finds me like that. they all give me the same look, and it's a look of pity. they all think 'oh poor you' like something happened to me. 'no, nothing happened, i'm just overthinking again.' i wish i'd said that.

i wonder what he thought when he opened the door and found me in the corner. i don't know if he'd ever noticed me before. he probably didn't even know i existed. he doesn't seem like the type who pays attention to anyone. whereas me, i notice everyone.

he probably would have helped more if he really cared though, so maybe that's good. maybe the fact that he walked off means he doesn't want anything to do with me. that's probably best. i don't want anything to do with him either.

that's what this feeling is. fear of him, of what he might think. dread perhaps. embarrassment that he saw me like that. the first time the guy i've loved for goodness knows how long ever really saw me i was in such a state.

no. i don't love him. and i never have. it's a stupid crush, just because he's so gorgeous, that's all. he's horrible, and i don't want anything to do with him. ever. i don't love him and i never have. and i sure as hell never will.

oh god. just look at the cobwebs. they're back now, focus on them. don't think of him.

what is happening?

i know damn right what's happening.

stop thinking.

look at the cobwebs.

i hate this feeling.

i want it all to go away.

pretty cobwebs.

why can't it stop? if only i could sleep, i wouldn't have to spend the nights thinking like this. i don't want anything to do with him, i *don't*.

look at the stars then.

not the stars. i've never hated them before but right now i can't stand the sight of them. stupid stars.

don't close the window.

i'm closing the window. i don't even care.

i like the sound the window makes as it closes. i've never thought about that before, but it's a satisfying noise.

there we go, distract yourself.

no, now i'm thinking about it again.

i need to stop.

i wish i could sleep.

my hands won't stop shaking.

i am afraid.

They

She didn't want to move.

He didn't want to stay still.

She wanted nothing more than silence.

He wanted nothing more than to walk again.

She'd spent her day lying on her floor, ignoring the world and thinking about life.

He'd spent his day sitting in his chair, wondering if it was possible to get his life back.

She had no enthusiasm left; the stress of life had got to her and she'd given up.

He had too much energy, and he only wanted to use it.

She watched the shadows run across her ceiling as the trees shook gently in the wind outside.

He watched the nurses wheel trolleys around to all the other patients, tending to their every need.

She listened to the creaking of the pipes as the water warmed them up and cooled them down.

He listened to the hushed murmurs of the other patients discussing god knows what.

She gave in to her exhaustion and closed her eyes.

He gave in to his temptation and called over a nurse.

She asked herself why she was still trying, and got no answer.

He asked the nurse if he could perhaps go out, who eventually said yes.

She was too tired.

He was too happy.

She went through the things that mattered to her, but the list was too short.

He went out into the garden in his wheelchair, admiring everything he saw.

She wondered how long it was until she didn't have to try.

He wondered how long it had been since he'd seen the outside world.

She heard someone downstairs calling her name.

He heard thunder rumble in the distance.

She ignored the voice, not wanting anything to disrupt her peace.

He ignored the sound, not wanting anything to ruin this experience.

She noticed the pipes had stopped creaking.

He noticed raindrops on the back of his head.

She shut out the world, ignoring the shouts and door slamming downstairs.

He shut out the rain and thunder, only focusing on what was good here.

She realised the house was silent suddenly, and wondered where everyone had gone.

He realised the wind was too strong, and struggled to keep control of his wheelchair.

She managed to haul herself off the floor and went downstairs to investigate.

He managed to pull himself close to the hospital and waited for somebody to come.

She couldn't scramble back up the stairs in time.

He couldn't see the wave until it was too late.

She tried to shut the door, but she knew it wouldn't work.

He tried to wheel away, but he knew it was hopeless.

She was soon up to her waist in water, which was still rising.

He was soon submerged by the wave, which knocked him out of his chair.

She struggled to keep her face above the water.

He struggled to swim using just his arms.

She realised it was pointless.

He realised he was dying.

She saw spots as her last breath left her body and bubbled up to the surface.

He saw his arms and legs floating above him; already he'd lost any sense of feeling.

She was surrounded by darkness which crept in through the corners of her eyes.

He was fading quickly, and he could feel himself losing consciousness.

She awoke lying on something soft.

He awoke to feel no pain.

She stood up and took in her surroundings.

He stood up and was amazed his legs worked.

She was standing on what looked like nothing, with her feet only just visible.

He was surrounded by white; there was no floor or walls, just light.

She saw him standing not far from her, and wondered who he was and why he was here.

He saw her looking around and wondered if she knew where they were.

She started walking over to him, figuring it was a safe bet.

He started walking towards her, hoping she'd have some answers.

She asked him where this place was and why they were here.

He asked her if she knew what was happening.

She laughed because they'd spoken at the same time.

He laughed because she'd laughed and he liked it.

She said she thought she'd drowned.

He said he thought he had too.

She told him her house had flooded.

He told her there was a storm.

She wondered if they were both dead.

He wondered if she was possibly right.

She admitted she was happy he was here.

He admitted he was happy he was here too.

She asked him why that was.

He asked her to explain first.

She reluctantly told him she'd heard people calling her and had ignored them because she wanted to be alone.

He reluctantly told her he'd been paralysed from the waist down and just wanted to experience the world again.

She realised it was her own fault she was here.

He realised his selfishness had caused his own death.

She knew that if she'd been in his situation she would have been fine.

He knew that if they'd swapped places they'd both be alive.

She thought they could help each other.

He thought they needed one another.

She held out her hand to his and could feel them merging.

He held her hand in his and watched as he and she became . . .

They.

They walked off in search of anybody to help them.

They let the soft ground beneath them envelop their feet.

They walked for days on end without finding anyone else.

They explored to every corner, but there was always somewhere they hadn't been.

They had no purpose, but they didn't mind.

They were happy.

They were glad to be alone.

They were glad to have legs.

They loved the peace.

They loved to walk.

But,

They had a problem.

They were always in an inner conflict.

They were too negative.

They were too positive.

They had no enthusiasm.

They had too much energy.

They were too tired.

They were too happy.

They didn't know what to do.

They always argued with themselves.

Because,

She didn't want to move,

and

He didn't want to stay still.

Hand in Hand

Thatch

"You're late," Alton growls as Cinder waltzes in half an hour after she agreed to meet us. Nobody's surprised. Cinder's always off doing her own thing, and more often than not, she doesn't tell anyone where she is.

"I know."

"You'd better've found something good, or you got no excuse again."

Cinder pulls a scrawny kid in through the door behind her.

"This is Shaunie."

Dagger and I snigger as Alton takes a step closer to Cinder.

"Wha's she doing here?" It's more of a threat than a question, and the tension between them makes the air quiver.

"She was alone. She'd survived one night but I didn't think she could stay there, not 'ow the streets've been recently."

Alton laughs, but there's nothing funny.

"What'd Taie think of all this then?" he says. "First Dagger, now this thing?"

"Hey if you got a problem, Alton—" Dagger stops as Alton spins round and grabs him by the collar.

"Yeah? Maybe I do."

"Guys stop!" I stand up and both of them flinch a little at the tone of my voice. I'm the peacekeeper; although nobody's ever said it it's become my role. When I want attention I get it.

"What'd Taie think of *this*?" I ask, gesturing to the two boys grabbing at each other's throats. "She wasn't a racist, as you know. She was fine with Dagger, she'd be fine with this." I turn to Alton. "You know you're technically doing the same as what they did to you."

Alton looks surprised for a moment, then he drops Dagger and regains his usual aggressive self. He points a finger at Shaunie.

"You better behave, kid. Or I'm kickin' your ass back out into the cold."

There's a tense silence as Shaunie trembles under Alton's gaze.

"It's gonna snow tomorrow," Cinder says suddenly, breaking the silence.

"We'll assume you brought supplies to keep us warm, then?" Dagger sneers. "Since you knew in advance and all."

"There wasn't much. Seems everyone wants warm clothes now."

"Well I wonder why that is," Alton says sarcastically, rolling his eyes. "If we freeze in 'ere, it's your fault."

"At least she warned us," I say. "We can go get stuff now."

Alton sighs, realising I'm right and I can see how much he hates it.

"Fine."

"Thatch, you and Shaunie stay here," Cinder says. "We need someone to watch out and Shaunie could do with some rest."

"You're stickin' with us though," Dagger tells Cinder. "No wanderin' off and bringin' more children back with you."

Cinder rolls her eyes and they make their way to the door.

"If anyone comes, you know what to do," Alton says before he closes the door behind them.

I turn to Shaunie once I lose the sound of their footsteps outside.

"Sorry about them. I guess this is all a bit confusing."

She shrugs. "It isn't much more chaotic than my house always was."

"Did your parents fight a lot?"

Shaunie tilts her head a little. "Not really. It was my Dad and Stepmum arguing with my Dad's parents. They were always arguing."

"What were they arguing about?"

"Me."

"Why?"

"My Dad's always accepted me for who I am, and so has my Stepmum. He divorced my real Mum when I was thirteen because she hated me, but he can't get away from my grandparents."

"I'm sure they don't hate you."

"They do."

She looks so forlorn then that I almost don't want to ask any further, in case I upset her. But curiosity and boredom get the better of me and I find myself saying the next two words despite my promise not to.

"How come?"

"I used to be a boy."

She looks at me then, right in the eye and I see that hers are young and blue and so innocent. She doesn't deserve this. Seeing the tears form I pull her into a hug and her body feels so small. She can't be very old, I decide; fifteen maybe? She has too much life left to be here.

I suddenly feel very angry for her, for everything she's been through. I want to make it all right again, for all of us, but I know I'll never be able to do that. It's at that moment that I first realise quite how much I miss Taie.

Alton

The air is already frosty as we head out, and the sun has set behind the mountains in the distance.

"I guess tha's good," Cinder says when I point this out. "Less chance of anyone recognising us."

"Yeah, but what 'appens when our bloody toes freeze off?" Dagger moans. "I dunno bou' you but I wanna go home with all my body parts please."

We ignore his comment and carry on.

My feet crunch on frost as we shiver our way over to the shopping centre. On the way we find eighty six pence on the floor in various places, and added to the coins we've collected during the week we decide we have enough for a cheap blanket. It's not much, but unless we want to break Taie's golden rule of not stealing unless completely necessary, it's all we can get.

The first flake of snow falls just as we're leaving the shop. It lands on Dagger's shoulder and I glare at Cinder.

"Thought it wan't s'posed to snow till tomorrow," I say smugly.

"That's what I heard," she says, her voice barely audible.

"Well you heard wrong didn't you." I take a step towards her, enjoying the way she shrinks under my gaze. Cinder may be the oldest, but she's still scared of me.

"Alton, stop," Dagger says, grabbing my shoulder. "We need to go."

I'm about to snap at him when I see where he's looking. The mountains on the horizon have disappeared under huge dark clouds which roll across the ground, and by the looks of it they carry more than just a few flakes. Dagger's right. We need to get back, now.

Cinder starts running and we follow. Wind pushes us in the opposite direction and tiny shards of ice beat at my face. Before long the air is completely grey and I can barely see the other two, and even if I shout they probably wouldn't hear. Besides, I can't do that. Shouting would show fear, and I can't be afraid.

Waving my hands around I find the edge of a building and manage to find a sort of shelter in an indent in the wall. Only once I'm reasonably safe do I panic. Cinder and Dagger aren't with me. I search for them in the snow, but it's too dark, and all I can make out are a few moving shapes. I don't even know if they're people or not.

Then I stop myself. This isn't like me. I'm not supposed to care; I'm the designated asshole of the group. I'm not the nanny, that's Thatch. They can take care of themselves. I'll probably get back and find they've been there this whole time. Yeah.

Somebody opens a door not far from where I'm stood. A figure stands in the light from whatever room is behind the door, and they beckon to me.

"Come on," the figure says, and I find my legs taking me towards them.

Once I'm inside I see the figure is a boy, a little shorter than me, probably younger. His sandy blond hair and blue eyes remind me of Shaunie, the little git. That and the fact he's white. He doesn't seem to care though, and he smiles at me as I stand there, shivering.

"Who's this?"

I turn and see an older man coming in through a door at the back of the room. He walks around the counter and I realise we're in a shoe shop, and he must be the owner.

"It's cold outside," the boy says, "and he was just standing there."

"Get it out."

It. Not even *he*. I'm just *it*.

I feel my fists tense at my side.

"I'll go," I say hesitantly, and I find myself very glad the others aren't here with me. I'm way out of my comfort zone at the moment.

"No, it's fine," the boy says, and turns back to the man. "It's snowing outside. Really heavily. He can't survive just in that." He gestures to the thin clothes I'm wearing.

"I said get it out my shop!" the man shouts, almost saying each word as an individual sentence.

"Dad, stop." The boy moves to stand between me and the older man.

"Get out you filthy nigg—"

My fist is in his face before he can finish the word. The word I haven't been called for six years but which has the exact same effect. The man looks shocked for a second before he punches me back. I taste blood as he pushes me into the wall behind me, slamming my head against the glass of the window. The room spins around me and I'm about to hit him in some way, when he opens the door and literally kicks me out the shop.

I sit in the snow for a while, because I don't have the energy to move and because I feel so pathetic. I feel sick and my head is pounding, and all I can think is that this is what I threatened to do to Shaunie. I don't know where the thought comes from, it's just there. I think of what Thatch said, *you're technically doing the same as what they did to you*. Maybe I have been too unfair.

Eventually I drag myself up from the floor. I can't tell if I'm weak from the fight or if my clothes are just so sodden I'm heavier than usual, but it seems to take a lot of effort to stand. It's a little easier to see now, so I begin to trudge my way through the snow.

I have never wanted to see that crumbly building more than I do now.

Shaunie

"So, have you managed to keep track of everyone here?" he asks, once he's finished showing me around the building. It's an old house, some of the walls barely thick enough to keep the wind out, but it's the best they have.

"I think so. You're . . ." I stop, not sure if I remember his name.

"Thatch," he says, chuckling. "Though I wouldn't expect you to remember that. It's not like anyone screamed my name or anything."

"I know Cinder though. And Dagger, and Alton."

"That's good."

We're both silent for a bit, before I speak again.

"Why are you called Thatch?"

"It's not my real name. Though you'd probably guessed that. Taie said we should change our names so that we could properly let go of our past and move on. I don't know if it worked, but it made sense."

"Shaunie isn't my name either."

He turns to look at me then, as if he's trying to see whether I'm telling the truth.

"Isn't it?"

"No. Cinder asked what my name was and I just made one up. I guess it felt wrong, telling a stranger what my name was as soon as we met. And I've always had a boy's name. I wanted her to know I was a girl."

He nods but doesn't say anything. I remember another question I was going to ask and try to work out how to phrase it.

"How come you're all scared of Alton?"

"We're not," he says, frowning, and I think maybe he is genuinely confused.

"You all listen to what he says. Cinder seemed scared as she opened the door when we arrived. It looks like he's in charge of you all."

"Yeah, of course you'd think that."

"What d'you mean?"

"There wasn't ever supposed to be anyone in charge. The deal was we all worked together to stay alive and protect each other. But lately we've all become a little more . . . aggressive, Alton in particular."

"Why's that?"

"He likes to think he's tough, but I think he was affected a little more by Taie's death than the rest of us were, and definitely more than he lets on."

I remember the name from when Cinder explained where she was taking me.

"Is Taie the woman who looked after you?"

"Yeah. Did Cinder tell you about her?"

"A little. How did she die?"

As soon as I've asked the question I wonder if I've gone too far. Thatch takes a shaky breath and sits up straight.

"We don't know exactly. Some men came to the house and took her. We all managed to escape but I think I heard gunshots as we ran. It was a few days before we thought it safe to return to the house and when we did, she wasn't here. It was in a bit of a state but we managed to clean it up just enough." Thatch gestures miserably to the worn cottage we sit in.

"Why did they take her?"

"She was a white woman looking after black children that weren't hers." He laughs bitterly. "This country is messed up."

I want to know more, but at the same time I don't want to upset him. I'm trying to think of a way to change the subject when he sighs and continues talking.

"Taie found Alton first, that's why he was so attached to her I guess. His family were thrown out of their home when he was fourteen, and he lost them. Taie found him and took him in, because she didn't agree with any of it. This was her home."

"What about the others?"

"Cinder joined them three years later. She was eighteen and wasn't allowed a place in college because of her skin colour, so she ran away. She found Taie a little while before she actually went to stay with them, and was suspicious at first. But it didn't take her long before she realised she needed them."

"And Dagger?"

"His Dad was shot while they were in town. His mother told him to run so he did, and Taie took him in three days later."

"Why?" I ask. "Why all the violence?" But I'm beginning to see a pattern now and I almost dread the answer he'll give me.

"Dagger's Dad was black. And his Mum was white."

"That's why Alton doesn't like him."

"Alton doesn't think Dagger qualifies to be with us, since he isn't fully black. But in the eyes of some people, being mixed is even worse."

"Is that why Alton hates me then?"

Thatch hesitates, as though he doesn't want to answer.

"Yeah," he says eventually. "You're the first white kid who's stayed with us."

Dagger

When we finally get back to the house we're shivering and sneezing, and my hair is stuck to the back of my neck by a sort of slushy snow that's refrozen, and the blanket is so wet it wouldn't do much good, and Cinder cries because it's "all so bloody pointless", and Shaunie just sits and looks terrified through the whole thing.

Alton doesn't get back until very late. As the door opens we all jump up, half expecting a stranger to walk in. And it practically is a stranger that shuts the door behind him and winces under a fierce hug from Cinder.

Alton's eye is bruised and his lip is bleeding. He limps over to the ledge we usually sit on and slowly lowers himself down next to Thatch. Shaunie looks like she wants to say something; I think we all do, but we know exactly what happened.

"It's fine," Alton says gruffly. "Just got into a fight."

We don't need any more explanation. We all know why Alton gets into fights. It was the same last time, and the time before.

"Who was it?" Cinder asks.

"Some shop owner. I dunno where I was 'cause of the snow."

"What'd he say?"

"It was only half a word. But I don't care."

"Alton, people are going to say things," Thatch says. "You can't keep getting into fights like this. It draws attention to us."

"You think attention in't already on us? All you gotta do is walk down the bloody street and people are starin'. Attention's always gunna be on us, no matter what I do."

"Just listen to him," I say. "He has a point."

"I don't want you talkin' to me," Alton growls, standing up and pointing a bruised finger at me. "I don' care what colour your Dad was, your Mum was one o' them and so are you."

"Alton . . ." Cinder starts, but I shake my head at her. Alton always says things like his when he's angry. He never really means anything, no matter what he thinks.

"And I want her out!" he shouts at Shaunie. "She causes nothing but trouble."

"How is it her fault it snowed?"

"Not just the snow, everything. She stays, an' one or more of us are gunna get killed. Get out."

With that he turns and storms up the stairs. There's nothing up there except a few empty rooms with holes in the walls, but he doesn't seem to care and none of us feel like telling him.

"I'll go talk to him," Cinder says.

"I dunno if tha's a good idea," I say.

"It'll be fine, trust me. Jus' wait here."

The three of us are silent for a bit after she leaves, and I can't help but worry what Alton will say, or do, since she's in there on her own with him.

"I don't like the world much," Shaunie mutters after a while.

"Don't you?" Thatch says.

"No. It's too cruel and everybody hates each other."

Thatch and I share a look that I don't entirely understand, and I have to look away from both of them.

"Will I be allowed to stay with you?" Shaunie asks.

"Of course you will," Thatch says. "Ignore Alton, he's just angry."

"Don't you have anyone?" I ask.

Shaunie shakes her head. "There aren't even any 'missing' posters up. I don't think anybody really misses me."

"Well we would, okay?" Thatch puts his arm around her. "So don't listen to Alton. You can stay with us."

Shaunie smiles and leans her head against his shoulder. We stay like that then and don't talk until Cinder emerges, Alton sulking behind her. He still looks to be in a bad mood but at least she's got him out.

"Let's go," she says.

"What?"

"We're leaving, grab everything if you can." Cinder's eyes are wide and hopeful as she says this, and I know it's something good. We're not running away; we're starting again.

Since we don't have much between us we manage with a little rucksack each. Nobody speaks as we pack, and although I know we're probably all wondering where we're going, not one of us asks. Cinder looks happier than I've seen her in a while, and I silently wonder what she's got planned.

"I'm gunna miss this place," Cinder says as we stand outside looking at it, flakes of snow floating around our heads. It's slowed down a bit now, so we're able to see a little more and there's less chance of any of us getting separated from the rest.

"We're not comin' back," Alton says. "Say goodbye and le's leave."

"Yeah." Cinder turns around and sighs. "Le's go then. Alton, you lead the way."

Cinder

By the time we reach the shop it's stopped snowing and our feet make crunchy prints in the fresh layer. We'll have to be quick; the sun will be rising soon and people will start to wake up and see us. I pull my hood tighter over my face as we approach the shop, and it's just what I'd hoped for. It's on the end of a terrace, so one wall is completely bare.

I dump my stuff down and turn to Shaunie, who's wearing a spare bandana I lent her just in case. Even though she's not as well known around here as the rest of us, I still didn't want to risk anything.

"Gimme your hand," I say.

Shaunie reaches her hand out tentatively, looking terrified as usual. I grab her hand in the end, probably being more rough than I should but I'm beginning to lose patience. We don't have much time.

"There," I say. "Tha's perfect." It's then that I realise she's holding my right hand, and I need it to do what I'm about to do.

"Um, Thatch, will you hold her hand?"

Thatch looks confused, as does Shaunie, but he does as he's told. It probably looks better with his hand, I decide, and reach in my bag for the brown bottle. Thatch's eyes grow wide and understanding, like he's worked out what I'm doing, and he smirks slightly.

I shake the bottle and put it up against the wall where I want to paint. I do Thatch's hand first, painting the shape in the lighter brown then going back over to do shadows with a darker colour. I mix the white with some brown to make a light shine on his fingers, deciding it looked too dark without. I want this to be as happy and positive as possible.

I do Shaunie's hand with the peachy colour, starting by painting her fingers in the gaps I've left in Thatch's hand. Then her palm emerges from behind, and her wrist ends in the same faded way Thatch's does. I shade and highlight it the same as I did his, then I take the white bottle. I paint a smudgy cloud-like circle around the hands, then make it fade into blue with the last bottle I'll be using. The hands seem to glow, and that's exactly the effect I was after.

The others have been silent as I was painting, but now I stand back and look at them all, wanting their opinions.

"It's great, as usual, Cinder," Dagger says, and the others nod in agreement. I look at Shaunie, and her face is shining. She has a huge grin on her face, and when she sees me looking she lets go of Thatch's hand and comes over to give me a big hug.

"That'll make 'em cross, won't it?" I say, and it will. A white person, hand in hand with a black person? Even in a painting they'd find it extremely offensive, and that's exactly what I want. They won't know whose hands they are, and it doesn't matter. All I want is for them to pay for what they did to Alton, and this way, they will. My paints don't come off easily.

Before we go, I sign the bottom of it. I don't even care if they know it was me. By the time somebody sees it, we'll be gone. And it's not like they'll care enough to follow us.

"And now we run," I say, pulling my bandana tighter over my face. People will be getting up soon. I check all the windows of the surrounding houses, and am relieved to see they're all dark. Nobody's seen us, yet.

I turn and head off down the alley between the shop and the house next to it, which is wide enough that people will see my painting as they pass. It couldn't have worked out any better. I smirk to myself. I hope they hate it. Shouldering my bag I start to run, and I can hear the footsteps behind me quicken as the others all follow. We won't be there to see people's reactions, but I can imagine them just well enough.

People will hate us, and I love that.

Five Stages

You'll wait for ages for him to show.

The clock will do nothing to aid your anxiety, insisting on reminding you repeatedly that it's been ten, twenty, thirty minutes since he should have come home. By the time it's been a full hour you'll lose your patience with the clock, picking it up and hurling it at the wall. It will bounce off and land on the kitchen work surface, completely unharmed and still ticking happily. You won't be able to understand how it can be so happy at this point in time.

You'll pick up your phone, scrolling through the various news stories that have popped up recently, barely reading the headlines. It'll be something to pass the time more than anything else. You'll read the headline about a car accident, and skip over it just like the rest. Then you'll realise what it said, and go back, heart pounding. The story won't be very detailed, since it's very new, but it'll tell you about how three cars have been involved in an accident, on the road he comes home along from work.

Your five-year-old daughter will push the door open, distracting you momentarily from any worries you may have. Her nighty that's too long for her will be slightly damp, and she'll hold an empty mug in her hand.

"I spilt my milk," she'll say.

"So you did." You'll reach for a piece of kitchen roll and mop up her dress, taking the mug from her and putting it by the sink to wash up later.

"Why are you crying?" she'll ask.

You won't have realised you were, but you'll wipe your eyes finding that they are in fact wet with tears.

"It's nothing," you'll say, not wanting to worry her.

There will be a pause as you dry her dress, but when you're done she'll break the silence by saying, "Where's Daddy?"

You'll fumble with the tissue in your hand, almost dropping it. You'll hesitate, trying to think of something - anything - to tell her other than the truth. In the end you'll decide that you have to be slightly honest, even if you don't tell her what you think has happened.

"He's- late," you'll say, just managing to force the words out.

"Well when he gets home tell him to come say goodnight to me."

You'll nod and take her up the stairs, not trusting your own voice to speak. You won't want to even think of the possibility that he might not come home at all.

Once she's in bed, you'll go back downstairs and curl up on the sofa, trying your best to ignore the bare spot beside you where he should be. You'll check the news again, and wish you hadn't. The website will have been updated, and now they'll have descriptions of the cars involved. You'll see the model of his car written on the screen, the pixelated letters staring you in the face, mocking you. Your heart will thump against your ribcage, threatening to burst out, and you'll pray more than anything that he's okay.

When the policeman arrives, you'll be reluctant to open the door. You will have been waiting for him, but at the same time, you'll hate to see him standing there. You'll hope that what he has to say is good news, but you'll know it's far from that when he begins talking.

"Ma'am, I'm sorry."

Your breath will catch in your throat, and you'll hardly need to hear what he says next, as he confirms that your husband is, in fact:

"Dead."

•••

Denial

You'll wake your daughter up earlier than you usually do the next morning, partly because you've been unable to sleep and partly because you think she ought to know. She'll rub her eyes and glare at you, as though she knows it's early even though she can't read the time. This will make you feel guilty, but you can't give up.

You'll sit her down at the breakfast table and get her a bowl of cereal to put off the inevitable conversation you'll be about to have.

"Daddy didn't come in last night," she'll say, causing your hands to shake and the milk to tip out faster than you expect. You'll hand her the flooded cereal and hope she doesn't guess anything's up.

"Daddy isn't here."

She'll eye you suspiciously and you'll curse her intelligence.

"Where is he?"

"I don't know." You'll sit opposite her and take her tiny hand. "Nobody knows, but he's probably okay and hopefully he'll be home soon."

She'll nod and you'll wonder how much she's holding back.

"So it's going to be okay. Okay?"

She'll pull her hand away from yours and glare at you, taking a mouthful of her cereal.

"When he gets back, he has to say goodnight to me for all the nights he's missed."

With that she'll stand up and leave.

"Where are you going?" you'll call.

You'll hear her voice call "it's too soggy," from another room and then a door will shut.

You'll clear up her bowl, sighing to yourself. *But at least I've told her the truth*, you'll remind yourself. *Children need to understand when this kind of thing happens. And anyway, he'll be back soon, and it'll all go back to normal.* You'll smile sadly to yourself and wish time would speed up so he'll get home.

•••

Anger

She'll walk up to you while you're sitting on the sofa, watching some crappy programme on the television. You won't have been fully paying attention; instead you'll have been too busy listening to your screaming thoughts.

"Mummy," she'll say.

"Not now sweetie." You'll wave her away without even seeing what she wants.

"But I need help. And you're not watching the telly anyway."

You'll wonder vaguely how she knows, before pressing the off button on the remote and turning to her. She'll be holding two jigsaw pieces in her hand, and you'll see that they've been forced together even when they obviously don't fit. You'll sigh and take the pieces from her, wrenching them apart and handing them back.

"Thank you. Can you help me with the rest?"

Deciding you have nothing better to do, you'll follow her up the stairs to her bedroom. About fifty jigsaw pieces will be scattered around the floor, making it almost impossible to move around the room. She'll have put a few together, but the rest will cover every available foot space. You'll find somewhere and sit down, facing her as she searches through the mess for a piece that fits.

"This is what they're doing for Daddy," she'll say after a while. "Looking through all the clues to find some that fit. The picture at the end will be him, then."

You'll stare at her, wondering where all that came from. *Is this why she wanted to do the jigsaw?* You'll ignore her little statement, trying to carry on with the jigsaw. You'll both be silent for a while before she rolls onto her back and declares she's bored.

"You haven't done very much, Mummy," she'll say, studying the pieces that have been put together.

"Well it's your jigsaw. You're supposed to be doing it."

"Daddy always does it for me."

"Well Daddy isn't here." You'll slot a piece in with your shaking fingers as she continues to roll around on the floor, messing up the pieces which you'd carefully arranged.

"You could still do it for me. You could be like Daddy and Mummy while he's not here. Then when he gets back you can —"

"Daddy's not coming back!" you'll shout. You will have lost your patience with her, and the bloody jigsaw. You'll throw the piece you have in your hand at the floor, not even caring that it'll mess up your order.

"But you said . . ."

You'll feel slightly bad, but you can't explain to her. She won't understand.

"Daddy's gone, and he's not coming back."

You'll stand up and storm out of her room, leaving her sitting in amongst scattered jigsaw pieces, tears shining in her eyes.

•••

Bargaining

She'll find you crouched on the floor, face down on the bed, sobbing. She'll take your hand and hold it, not saying anything, as though she knows that's exactly what you'll need. You'll smile at her and wonder, how could the world be so cruel to her? *Maybe if things were different she could have a bright future.* You'll imagine all the smiles and happiness in that girl's future, and you'll laugh out loud at how different it looks. All you'll be able to see for her now is this.

You'll wonder what you could have done differently, if there's a way you could make it all better for her. You'll wonder if you should have done more, to help her and to help him. Perhaps you should have known that road was dangerous. *Perhaps he should have known . . .*

Was there a driver at fault? If so, was it him?

You'll find any way to blame anybody but yourself, because deep down you'll know it was your fault. You'll want to blame him, your daughter, the man who brings the post in the mornings. You'll want to blame them all in turn before realising none of them had anything to do with it. But for some reason, you won't be able to convince yourself that *you* had nothing to do with it.

"Daddy's happy where he is," she'll say after a while, still holding your hand. "Mrs Briggs says good people go to heaven when they die, and Daddy was a good man. He'll be happy."

You won't want to tell her that you don't believe in heaven, because once she's said that, you'll want more than anything for it to be true. You'll pray for the first time since you were her age that night, begging God to make sure he's happy, and to protect her from any harm. You won't ask for anything for yourself, because at the moment, you'll be the least of your worries.

•••

Depression

You'll be lying in bed when she knocks on the door and comes in without waiting for you to give her permission.

"Mummy," she'll say. "I'm hungry."

You'll sigh. "Well, you should have eaten your breakfast then. You said it was too soggy."

"But . . . that was yesterday."

"Was it?" You'll struggle to remember.

"You didn't wake me up either."

You'll rub your forehead, trying to soothe the headache you've had since the police came.

"I've had trouble sleeping, sweetie. We'll get up now if you like."

You'll stand up and open the curtains, letting light flood the room. Normally you'd be delighted to see the outside world, but now all you'll be able to see is the world that killed your husband and left your five year old daughter fatherless.

Good people go to heaven when they die, and Daddy was a good man. He'll be happy.

You'll stare up at the sky. Oh yes, of course *Daddy* will be happy. Trust *Daddy* to leave the two of us here while he's off being the good man he is. If *Daddy* is such a good man, why can't he just come back?

Your daughter will walk slowly over to you and you'll realise you said all that out loud. She'll put her arms around you and cry into your pyjamas, and you'll feel her pain for the first time. You won't have stopped to think how much this has affected her; you'll have been too caught up in your own pain to worry too much about her. For the first time, you'll realise you've probably been too hard on her. For the first time, you'll realise you haven't been there when she needed you most.

For the first time, the thumping in your head will relent.

•••

Acceptance

It won't come easily. By the time you've accepted his death you will have moved house and gone through several of the other stages once, maybe even twice more. But it will come. You'll be sitting in a chair in the garden of your new house, and she'll come over to you. By this time she'll be six, having had her birthday a few days ago; you were relieved when she told you she didn't want a party. She'll be clutching some new toy she got as she strolls over.

"Mummy," she'll say.

"Yes, sweetie?" You'll turn to her and smile, and it'll be a real smile, too. Not like all the ones you've faked for so long, a real, happy smile. She'll notice, and grin back.

"I need help."

She'll hold out her toy, and you'll see it's a box containing a jigsaw. But not like any other jigsaws she's had, this one will be 3D. The finished picture will be a globe, with pictures of that cartoon she keeps watching. Your smile will get even wider, if possible, and you'll stand up to follow her.

"Daddy always did it for me," she'll say, a cheeky glint in her eye.

"Well I'm not Daddy, am I? So you'll have to help. You're a big girl now, anyway. Aren't you?"

She'll stop, a thoughtful look on her face.

"Yes," she'll say eventually. "I'm a big girl, and I won't get bored."

She'll open the back door determinedly, leading you up to her room. Once you're in she'll open the box and spill the pieces everywhere, and you'll notice they're numbered on the back.

"You put them in order," she'll say, "and I'll put them together."

"Deal," you'll say, before getting to work.

Another Girl

The bus is deadly silent as it takes us towards whatever sticky end will meet us at the other side. The girl next to me chatters on about anything she can think of, but I'm not listening. Her chatter doesn't help the silence; if anything, it only intensifies the more she talks. The air is thick with unspoken words, and no amount of small talk can comb through the knots of dread that hang around us.

I've done this journey many times before, and each time it's the same. There's always a bus, there's always a girl, and there's always a silence.

The girl this time goes by the name of Elouise. She's not unlike any of the other girls. All the Janes, Rachaels and Freyas were just as unknowing as her, and they all talked to fill the silence. Elouise carries on explaining what she can see out the bus window to herself, or maybe it's to me. I don't listen, even if the latter is true. I don't need to know what she sees.

The bus rushes past yet another stop without waiting to see if anyone is getting on or off. The driver knows nobody is - Elouise and I are the only people on the bus and nobody's waiting at any of the stops. Everybody got off when we arrived, as they always do.

Elouise points out that it's started raining outside, as it has. She goes on to describe the sky and the clouds and anything she can see, just so she can say something. I want to tell her to stop, but I know she probably finds the silence so much more unbearable than I find her. Besides, I'm not allowed to talk yet.

A hand brushes up against the back of my neck, reminding me that there isn't much time left. I don't need the reminder; I can feel the minutes slipping by as surely as I can feel the hairs on the back of my neck prickle and stand on end. Elouise stops talking and looks over in my direction. Clearly she's noticed something.

"What is it?" she asks.

I shake my head, my mouth having gone dry. I put my hands under my legs to stop them trembling, but not until after she sees. She touches my arm gently and I pull away, trying to ignore the searing pain her fingers have left.

"Talk to me, Otis. Where are we going?"

She stares at me for a little while longer before giving up and turning back to the window, but this time she doesn't talk. The miserable weather combined with my mood must have rubbed off on her. I feel bad for her, as I always do, but it's her or me. I have to do this.

The hand pats me on the head as if to reassure me that my thoughts are correct. It then proceeds to slide down the side of my face and cup my chin, turning my head towards the front of the bus.

"Lou," I say. "We're here."

From now on I'm allowed to talk, but I still have to be careful about what I say. If Elouise realises what's happening she could run, and then I'd be in the deepest of trouble. She stands up and follows me off the bus, thanking the driver on her way.

We stand in the rain by the bus stop for a while, before Elouise speaks.

"Are we going?"

I nod and lead her in the right direction. Our feet make soft splashing noises in the puddles along the pavement, but all I can focus on is the extra set of splashes. Elouise won't be able to hear them yet, but I know we're being followed. The worst part is I know who it is and what they want.

There was a time when I needed help finding the clearing, but by now I've done this so many times I know exactly which trees we pass as we turn off the pavement and into the woods. Here the earth is slightly drier, but that won't be true for long. It needs to be soaking for this to work. That's why he made it rain.

"Hurry up, Otis," a voice hisses in my ear, and the hand that belongs to it lightly strokes my hair. "I'm getting impatient."

I gulp and nod, quickening my pace. Elouise notices and copies me.

"Where are we going?" she asks again.

"You'll see. It'll be fine."

"You don't seem like it'll be fine. You look worried."

"Do I?" I'm aware that I'm probably talking too fast, but I can't stop myself. "What makes you think that?" My breath comes in pants and it's hard to talk in between them.

"We're almost running."

I stop suddenly. She's right, I had been running. I hesitate to catch my breath before remembering he's here.

"We can't stop, we have to go."

"Why? What's rushing us?"

I ignore her and carry on towards the clearing.

"Otis, please explain."

"I can't," I shout, turning to face her. I sigh and try again. "I can't. Just . . . trust me."

I realise as I say it that even if she decides to it'll cost her. She doesn't have a choice at this point, whether she knows or not. Whatever she does now will cost her life. Unaware of the danger ahead, Elouise agrees and follows me.

We arrive at the clearing within a couple of minutes, thankfully. It's exactly as it's always been, since it's probably in too deep for anyone to find by accident. The place has a sinister air about it, and Elouise seems to notice. She paces around, looking up and down nervously as though checking for something that will jump out at her. I almost want to laugh because the thing she's looking for is right behind me, and has been the whole time.

"Ah, Elouise. How lovely of you to come."

Elouise turns to face the figure that's been following us all the way here.

"Thank you, Otis," he says. "You've been very helpful, but I won't need you now."

He flicks his wrist and my legs are forced to walk out of the way.

"Otis," Elouise stammers. "What's going on?"

The figure glares at me and a tear trickles down my face, a combination of guilt and the pain his gaze causes me. I can't save her now. I've brought her here and now I don't need to watch. It's her or me after all.

Elouise trembles as the figure paces in a circle around her. He examines her, seeing if she lives up to his expectations. Clearly she does, because he stands back and she falls to her knees.

"You're a sweet girl, Lou," he says, rubbing his forehead. "I would apologise, but I don't feel any regret. How old are you right now?"

Elouise gulps. "Fourteen."

"Fourteen. Fourteen *years*. You see? Fourteen whole years you've been on this earth. That's plenty of time to have experienced the world, as you have. Your family loves you, you do well in school, you have friends. Your life has been fine, but, unfortunately for you, it's time for it to end."

"What?"

"Shh, shh." He holds up a hand to silence her. "I know what you're thinking, Lou. I can see exactly what you think. But you see, I can't just pick someone with a horrible life as it is. I find, if the child wants to die, then it's not as much fun. Yes, I know. That might sound horrible to you, but I have to have someone. And if your life has been worth it then little Otis here doesn't feel as guilty about bringing you to me."

She glances in my direction, looking almost as if she'd forgotten I was here. Her eyes are full of tears and she looks so betrayed. I feel awful for her, but I know it'll be over soon. I stare down at the log I'm leaning against to avoid looking her in the eye.

"So. I apologise on behalf of Otis, but I'm getting weak, and I need you." He rubs a hand over his face and sighs. "I'll try and make it as painless as possible. For the both of you."

With one look he sends Elouise falling onto her back, her breathing ragged and sobs shaking her body. He leans down towards her and opens his mouth, a sort of white mist coiling from her into him. I turn away so as not to have to watch, even though I know exactly what's happening. I made the mistake of watching the first time.

When he's done he sighs contentedly and comes over to stand by me. I still can't look up; the mere idea of Elouise's limp body sprawled on the forest floor makes me feel sick to my stomach. A cold hand is placed on my shoulder and he strokes my arm with his thumb.

"There, there," he says. He probably thinks he's being comforting, but he just sounds annoyed and slightly sarcastic. "Get up."

I stand up shakily, sniffing and wiping my eyes on the back of my sleeve.

"I kept my side of the deal," I mumble.

"Yes you did. And now for my agreement." He snaps his fingers and smiles. "There."

"Nobody will remember her?"

"Nobody. Her whole existence has been erased."

"And nobody will think I've done anything."

"Don't worry your pretty little head. Everything is fine. Now, you know the drill."

I nod slowly.

"You have one year. If I'm honest I'd like to take them more often; a year is a long time to wait and I find I'm not as pleasant to be around when I'm hungry. But, you need your time. Just make it quick, Otis. No dawdling. Make friends with her, get her to trust you, then bring her here. I'll be waiting."

I nod and make my way past him. I try my best to avoid looking at Elouise but I catch a glimpse of her as I pass.

"Close her eyes," I beg, feeling something rise up in my throat. I hear the footsteps behind me but I can't look to check if he's done it. Instead I leave him with her and trudge past all the right trees to find my way out of this horrid place. I cross the road at the edge of the forest as if nothing is wrong and catch the bus back home.

I ride the whole way back alone, Elouise's spirit leaning heavily on my conscience, adding to all the Janes and Rachaels and Freyas. She's just the same as them now. Just another girl who was unfortunate enough to trust me.

And now I'm off to find the next.

A Bird

A bird.
Sitting in a tree.
Sheltering from the rain
at midnight.

The bird shakes its wings occasionally,
sending droplets of water
flying everywhere
from the branch it sits on,
before tucking its head
in between its wings,
and returning to sleep.

A figure.
Sitting on the curb.
Drenched in rain
at midnight.

Oh.
It's me.

I stand up shakily.
The bird keeps its eyes on me
as I attempt to dry myself off,
laughing because it's dry,
inspecting me with those
beady
black
lenses
it keeps in its head.
Its cameras.
I'm sure it's watching me
for a reason,
spying on me
for somebody.

The tarmac scrapes my bare feet
as I drag them forwards.
For some reason my body
doesn't seem
to want to work;
I feel sluggish
and still half asleep
as I trudge down the road,
my damp clothes hanging off me
like ragged sacks trying their best
to contain me.
It doesn't work,
because here I am,
and they've done nothing.

The thin layer of water
glistens on the road,
rippling every time
a drip
drops
from the sky.
Above me
the source of the light shines,
reminding me how happy I should be
and how happy I'm not.
Strings of tiny lights hang

from lamp to tree to lamp
diagonally across the road.
Of course.
It's Christmas.

I jump,
startled,
to see somebody
standing in the middle of the road,
before realising,
yet again,
it's me.
I'm watching myself
from somewhere distant,
like I'm another person
observing.

There's a shout
from somewhere behind me.
People running.
I might be one of them,
but I don't know what I look like.
Would I recognise myself
if I walked past?
An odd thought,
but my brain is fuzzy;
thoughts are taking a while
to form,
and when they do
I'm not all that sure
they make sense.

There are still people
running and shouting,
and the figure who looks like me
is just
standing
in the middle of the road.
He doesn't seem to be
in any hurry
to go anywhere.

"For god's sake,
move!"

The figure's legs obey him
and I'm running.
Beams of light from torches
make the ground around me shimmer.
On another day,
I might stop to watch
the patterns,
but I can't stop now.
I don't know what they want,
or why they're chasing me,
all I know is
I can't
stop.

A car
pulls up on the curb
sending water splashing over me.
I don't care.
The sign on the top tells me
it's a taxi,
my way out.
I open the door
and clamber in,
getting the back seat wet
as I do so.

"Just go,"
I tell the driver.
"Where?"
"Anywhere!"

He doesn't question me further.
Instead slams his foot down
and we're off.
The car speeds down the road.
It's early morning
and it's Christmas,

so there's nobody in sight.

Except I glance out the window,
and my heart lurches
to see a black car
speeding after us.
They're coming.
I twist in my seat
to get a better view of the car.
Another taxi
following me.

The driver turns to face me briefly.
"Everything alright?"

He smiles.
His face is familiar
but not enough.
I can't tell who he is.
My breath quickens
as I start to panic.

"Stop!"

The driver does as I say,
pulling over onto the curb again.
I leap out
and he drives off,
not even asking me to pay him.
We've only come
a few hundred yards or so
after all.

The taxi following us has stopped
and someone gets out.
The car speeds off
and the figure looks up,
meeting my eyes as he does so.
My shoulders tense up,
then relax slightly
as I realise who he is.

Me,
again.
I watch the cars speed down the road,
as the two merge to one
before disappearing
altogether.

I take a step forwards
and so does the other figure.
We shake our heads,
on another day
this would seem beyond possible,
but today
we can't bring ourselves
to wonder about it.
We're too tired.

No,
I'm too tired.

Out of the corner of my eye
I can see them.
The ones who were shouting
and running,
the ones who are after me.
I freeze,
stuck in one position for a while,
paralysed by fear
before my instincts kick in
and suddenly
I'm running.
My legs feel weak and wobbly,
not used to this much movement.

To my left
another me is running.
I've recognised him for once.
He grins
and winks at me,
before spreading out his arms.
He seems to shrink as he runs,

his body contorting into
something else.
His arms turn flat and feathery,
his grow legs small and spindly
until they're too weak to support him
and he jumps.
He spreads out his wings,
which catch him
and he's flying along beside me.
A bird.

And then my legs are off the ground
and I'm following him,
flying.
We zigzag in between lamps and trees,
over and under the string lights,
swooping high above the clouds
and then right down low to the ground,
taking advantage
of the lack of cars on the road.
The fluttering
of multiple wings beating together
as we're joined by twenty,
thirty other birds.

We flock to a tree,
all landing on different branches
and sending little
droplets of water falling,
raining down below us.
I shake my wings
and I'm dry enough
to sleep.
My eyes are shutting themselves
as I settle down on a branch.

A bird.
Sitting in a tree.
Sheltering from the rain
at midnight.

I wake to a loud thudding noise
and a bright light in my eyes
that I can't see past.
It feels like I'm lying in a puddle,
because my back
and part of my arms and legs
are damp.
As the thudding continues
and my thoughts clear slightly,
I become aware of a dull pain
somewhere,
but I can't quite work out where it is.

There's a lot of murmuring
and people shifting around,
but I'm not quite present enough
to see what's going on.
The colours of everything around me
change from
green
to blue
to white,
but I can't distinguish the shapes.

I hear birds chirping,
and leaves rustling,
and wheels squeaking,
and machines beeping,
and doors slamming.
People muttering
and that continuous thudding that
hasn't
stopped
once.

His head feels heavy against the pillow,
and everything is still
too blurry for him to see properly.
He's lying on a bed
which is being pushed along
a brightly lit corridor.

The bed comes to a halt
and they try to help him out.
He sits up dizzily and—

No,
that's wrong.

I sit up dizzily,
and they help *me* to a chair
and *I'm* the one who mumbles:

"What's happening?"

And I'm the one they do tests on.
It's me they stick the wires to
and mutter about to each other.
I'm the one who sits on the chair
only half aware
of everything around him
as they try and figure out
what the hell is wrong with him.

It's my arm that's covered in blood,
my wound they poke and prod at,
and it's me who repeatedly tells them:

"No, I can't feel anything."

And then when I'm wheeled out
on a wheelchair
since my body is too weak
to do anything,
I'm the one who's repeatedly asked
what happened,
the one who always answers honestly.

"I have no idea."

And even though it looks like
somebody else,
I'm the one who

spends my days
sitting on a wooden chair
by a huge window,
and stares at the world outside.
I spend my days watching the tree,
the tree which looks so familiar
and yet I can't say why.
And the bird.
Sitting in the tree.
Sheltering from the rain
at midnight,
and in the day,
and when I wake up in the mornings.
All the time.

The bird that stares at me,
watching me,
laughing as I try to work out
what's going on.
It sits there,
and smirks,
And doesn't
leave me alone.
Ever.

Forget

SATURDAY, MARCH 3RD

BAILEY
Dria
00:26

BAILEY
You there??
00:30

BAILEY
Listen you can't be sleeping yet.
00:33

BAILEY
Please, I need to talk to you
00:35

DRIA
omg bailey what do u want
00:38

BAILEY
Good you're here.
00:38

DRIA
yh well noticed
00:38

DRIA
what is it im tryna sleep
00:39

BAILEY
Can you come pick me up?
00:39

DRIA
this late??
00:39

DRIA
what u been doing
00:39

BAILEY
I'll answer questions when you get here.
00:39

BAILEY
Can you come?
00:40

DRIA
i dunno
00:40

DRIA
where r u?
00:40

BAILEY
Yeah, about that...
00:40

DRIA
wtf
00:40

DRIA
i need to know if im coming for u
00:41

BAILEY
I don't exactly know
00:41

DRIA
ur kidding
00:41

DRIA
bailey
00:42

BAILEY
Yeah
0:42

DRIA
ur kidding me right?
00:42

BAILEY
...
00:42

DRIA
bailey for gods sake
00:43

BAILEY
I'd like to say I am joking
00:43

DRIA
but ur not..?
00:44

BAILEY
No
00:44

DRIA
send me ur location
00:44

BAILEY
-[LINK]-
00:45

DRIA
cant believe u
00:45

DRIA
omw ok
00:45

BAILEY
K
00:45

BAILEY
I owe you one
00:47

> **DRIA**
> yeh yeh u know ull never keep it
> **00:47**

BAILEY
:)
00:47

THURSDAY, MARCH 8TH

BAILEY
I need a favour
06:59

> **DRIA**
> what is it now
> **07:02**

BAILEY
Can I borrow your car
07:02

> **DRIA**
> whats wrong with urs
> **07:02**

BAILEY
Can I just borrow it
07:02

BAILEY
Only for a couple of hours or so
07:02

BAILEY
Please
07:04

DRIA
listen u said u owed me one
07:05

BAILEY
And you said I'd never keep it.
07:05

DRIA
ur inposible
07:05

DRIA
imposible
07:05

BAILEY
Having trouble?
07:06

DRIA
shut it nerd
07:06

BAILEY
I'm hurt
07:06

BAILEY
So can I borrow your car??
07:07

DRIA
idk that depends if ur gonna b nice to me or not
07:07

BAILEY
That might just be the longest message you've ever sent me.
07:07

DRIA
so thats a no about the car..
07:08

BAILEY
Please I need it
07:08

BAILEY
Just for a couple of hours
07:08

BAILEY
I promise I'll bring it back in one piece
07:08

BAILEY
Ok?
07:09

DRIA
fine
07:10

DRIA
but this is the last time im helpin u
07:10

BAILEY
Of course..
07:10

DRIA
hope ur happy imma have to walk now
07:11

BAILEY
Love you too
07:11

DRIA
wait does that mean ur not going 2 school
07:13

BAILEY
Take a wild guess
07:13

DRIA
ooh baileys skipping school
07:13

DRIA
like a badass
07:13

BAILEY
Surprised you know how to spell badass
07:13

DRIA
shut ur face and come get the car
07:14

DRIA
before i change my mind
07:14

BAILEY
Yes ma'am
07:14

FRIDAY, MARCH 9TH

BAILEY
Hi there, favourite person of all time
18:36

BAILEY
Have I ever told you how beautiful you are?
18:36

BAILEY
I don't think I say it enough
18:37

DRIA
what do u want
18:39

BAILEY
Me???
18:39

BAILEY
Why do you think I want something?
18:39

DRIA
bc ur being nice
18:40

BAILEY
Aren't I always nice?
18:40

DRIA
u think ur being funny?
18:40

BAILEY
No, ma'am
18:40

DRIA
dont call me that
18:40

BAILEY
Of course, whatever you ask
18:40

DRIA
look b im not in the mood
18:40

DRIA
besides how do u think marshall would like 2 hear u calling me beautiful
18:41

BAILEY
Ooh, the Marshall threat
18:41

BAILEY
Lemme guess, is he the reason you're so cranky today?
18:41

DRIA
no
18:42

BAILEY
Took you a long time to type those two letters
18:42

DRIA
shut up ok
18:43

DRIA
its none of ur business
18:43

BAILEY
Awe, but I enjoy hearing how your relationship is going
18:43

BAILEY
Makes me glad I'm single
18:43

DRIA
its going fine
18:44

BAILEY
Well that's no fun
18:44

DRIA
well how would u like to here that ur part of the problem
18:44

BAILEY
It's "hear"
18:44

DRIA
omg i dont care
18:45

DRIA
ive got a lot going on atm and ur not helping ok?
18:45

BAILEY
Well I'm sorry to hear that
18:45

BAILEY
But I doubt you're going to tell me so I can't help
18:45

BAILEY
And I don't think any of your little 'friends' will want to listen
18:45

DRIA
hey i know you dont like marshall but i dont need u to lecture me about it all the time
18:46

DRIA
and yes i know how to spell lecture
18:46

BAILEY
I'm proud
18:46

DRIA
ha
18:46

BAILEY
Look your not the only one with problems ok?
18:47

DRIA
*you're
18:47

DRIA
:)
18:47

BAILEY
There, did that make you feel better?
18:47

DRIA
u did that on purpose
18:47

BAILEY
yep
18:48

DRIA
dick
18:48

BAILEY
So will you help me now?
18:48

DRIA
thought u didnt want anything
18:48

BAILEY
But you knew I did
18:48

DRIA
well what
18:48

BAILEY
This is gonna sound weird
18:49

DRIA
as if ur other requests werent
18:49

BAILEY
Ok actually I have two things I want you to do
18:49

BAILEY
The first is I want you to turn autocorrect on
18:49

DRIA
why
18:49

BAILEY
Because it'll correct your apostrophes
18:49

DRIA
right..
18:50

BAILEY
But you won't have to do anything
18:50

BAILEY
So we'll both be happy
18:50

DRIA
what's the other thing
18:50

BAILEY
Yay you've started already
18:50

BAILEY
Yeah the other thing...
18:50

BAILEY
In the glove compartment of your car, there's a small package wrapped in brown paper. I need you to take it somewhere remote, like in the middle of the woods or somewhere, and burn it. Make sure there's none of it left by

the time you're done, so nobody knows you did anything. Ok?
18:52

DRIA
you're not gonna answer but still
18:53

DRIA
why?
18:53

BAILEY
You're right I'm not going to answer.
18:53

BAILEY
I can't tell you
18:53

BAILEY
Sorry
18:53

DRIA
why not
18:53

BAILEY
Just trust me
18:53

DRIA
that's kinda hard atm
18:54

DRIA
ur being rlly weird recently
18:54

BAILEY
I know and I'm sorry
18:54

BAILEY
Can you do what I asked?
18:55

DRIA
well, sure...
18:55

BAILEY
Thanks
18:55

BAILEY
Oh and it's probably best you don't tell anyone about anything that's happened with me lately.
18:55

BAILEY
Ok?
18:55

DRIA
ok..
18:56

MONDAY, MARCH 12TH

DRIA
u ok??
16:12

DRIA
bailey
16:13

> **DRIA**
> how stupid do u think i am?
> **16:15**

> **DRIA**
> it says ur online
> **16:15**

> **DRIA**
> come on talk to me
> **16:16**

BAILEY
What
16:16

> **DRIA**
> wow u didn't even use a question mark
> **16:16**

> **DRIA**
> something must be wrong
> **16:16**

> **DRIA**
> Why aren't you talking to me?
> **16:18**

> **DRIA**
> Look I'm talking proper for you.
> **16:19**

BAILEY
*properly
16:19

> **DRIA**
> couldn't resist huh
> **16:19**

DRIA
what's going on??
16:21

BAILEY
It's nothing to do with you
16:21

DRIA
yes it is
16:21

DRIA
it's everything to do with me
16:21

DRIA
last i saw u, u were on the floor with ur face covered in blood, and now u ignore me all day??
16:22

DRIA
what happened with u and marshall?
16:24

BAILEY
It doesn't matter.
16:24

DRIA
well i ended it with him
16:25

DRIA
just thought you'd want to know
16:25

BAILEY
Cool
16:25

DRIA
so?
16:25

DRIA
u gonna explain?
16:26

DRIA
bailey fgs
16:29

DRIA
where'd u go?
16:33

SATURDAY, MARCH 17TH

BAILEY
Dria
02:26

BAILEY
I dunno what to do
02:26

BAILEY
People know, Dria, I know they do
02:27

BAILEY
I can see them looking at me
02:27

BAILEY
It's distracting
02:27

BAILEY
This whole thing has just messed up my life
02:28

BAILEY
I can't sleep
02:28

BAILEY
Teachers have noticed my work quality has gone down
02:28

BAILEY
They keep reminding me I have to keep on track
02:29

BAILEY
That I have exams soon and need to do well
02:29

BAILEY
But I can't focus
02:29

BAILEY
I can't forget.
02:29

BAILEY
My mind won't let me do anything other than worry
02:29

BAILEY
I need to tell someone
02:30

BAILEY
But I feel like they'll take it the wrong way
02:30

BAILEY
So I'm going to tell you now
02:30

BAILEY
But you must remember it was an accident
02:30

BAILEY
And promise not to think of me any differently once you know
02:30

BAILEY
Actually forget it I can't do this
02:42

SUNDAY, MARCH 18TH

DRIA
bailey wtf???
09:46

DRIA
r u there?
09:49

DRIA
srsly u can't just drop this on me and then leave
09:57

DRIA
i'm gonna have to go but message me if you need to talk
10:04

DRIA
xx
10:06

MONDAY, MARCH 19TH

DRIA
i'm worried now b
15:52

DRIA
why weren't you in today?
15:52

DRIA
bailey please let me know you're okay
15:57

BAILEY
-[LINK]-
15:58

DRIA
where is that?
15:59

BAILEY
No idea
15:59

DRIA
want me to come pick you up?
15:59

BAILEY
no
16:00

DRIA
why not
16:00

BAILEY
I'm here for a reason
16:00

DRIA
stop this b
16:00

DRIA
please come back
16:01

BAILEY
I can't.
16:01

DRIA
what are you doing?
16:01

BAILEY
I'm in a park
16:01

BAILEY
A little kids' park
16:02

BAILEY
It's deserted though
16:02

BAILEY
Only me
16:02

BAILEY
Sat on a swing
16:02

BAILEY
For children
16:02

DRIA
bailey what are you doing??
16:03

BAILEY
Thinking
16:03

DRIA
about what?
16:03

BAILEY
Everything
16:03

BAILEY
Something I did
16:03

DRIA
what did you do?
16:03

BAILEY
I don't think I can tell you that
16:04

DRIA
bailey listen..
16:04

DRIA
when i burnt your package it opened slightly and i saw what was inside
16:04

BAILEY
Oh
16:04

> **DRIA**
> wasn't that your favourite shirt?
> **16:05**

BAILEY
Maybe it was, maybe it wasn't
16:05

BAILEY
It doesn't matter now
16:05

> **DRIA**
> why did it have blood on it?
> **16:05**

> **DRIA**
> was it yours bailey??
> **16:07**

BAILEY
What if it wasn't?
16:08

> **DRIA**
> then i'd want to know whose it was
> **16:08**

BAILEY
somebody.
16:08

BAILEY
Who you don't know
16:08

BAILEY
Who you don't need to worry about
16:08

> **DRIA**
> why not
> **16:08**

> **DRIA**
> b?
> **16:09**

BAILEY
Because he's gone
16:10

> **DRIA**
> what
> **16:10**

BAILEY
Left the world
16:10

BAILEY
and he's not coming back.
16:10

> **DRIA**
> why..?
> **16:10**

> **DRIA**
> bailey why
> **16:11**

> **DRIA**
> what did you do??
> **16:11**

DRIA
bailey???
16:14

DRIA
hello?
16:15

DRIA
bailey i'm on my way okay?
16:17

DRIA
don't go
16:17

SATURDAY, APRIL 8TH

DRIA
Now it's my turn for a sleepless night.
01:33

DRIA
I know I shouldn't be here
01:33

DRIA
It's not really helping me "forget"
01:34

DRIA
That's what they call it
01:34

DRIA
All the doctors, teachers, my parents
01:34

DRIA
They want me to "forget" you.
01:34

DRIA
I don't think I can do that
01:34

DRIA
I still dream about your face that day
01:35

DRIA
Oddly enough that was the scariest part of the whole thing
01:35

DRIA
Not finding out what you did
01:35

DRIA
Not even the realisation as I saw what was happening a second too late.
01:35

DRIA
The dreams have got worse again since your funeral.
01:38

DRIA
They'd settled down a bit and all the adults were a little more hopeful for me.
01:38

DRIA
But ever since I saw the coffin
01:38

DRIA
And knowing it contained your body...
01:39

DRIA
I can't.
01:40

DRIA
I miss you
01:40

DRIA
And.. I know you're not reading these
01:43

DRIA
But I wanted you to know why I broke up with Marshall.
01:43

DRIA
I think he probably beat you up because he was jealous
01:43

DRIA
Now maybe that's hopelessly wrong but I don't care
01:44

DRIA
But I realised he had just cause to get jealous
01:44

DRIA
Because although you were a pain in the arse at the best of times
01:44

DRIA
I loved you.
01:44

DRIA
And now this is the bit where you have to message me saying "*love"
01:45

DRIA
I know it probably takes a while to send messages from the grave.
01:49

DRIA
Don't worry
01:49

DRIA
I'll be here
01:49

DRIA
Waiting for you.
01:49

DRIA
xx
01:50

Waiting

The feather sits in a glass case on her desk, beneath the mirror on the wall which she insists never shows her the truth. It's electric blue in colour, and it shines and sparkles when the sun comes in through the window, streaming past the blinds which split the light into long rays across the room. It looks dull and ordinary now in the darkness of the night, and Elis wishes it would stay like that. People would ask her what it was if they saw it shine; they'd want to know its entire history as soon as they laid eyes on it, which is precisely the reason why nobody ever comes to the house. Or at least, one of the reasons.

She wonders if she'll ever see him again, and if she does, whether he'll have the bird with him. That was his promise, *I'll be back. I don't know how long it'll take but I'll be back, and I'll bring you the bird.* She'd sighed and giggled stupidly, completely in awe of him and his bravery, loving how romantic it all was. She'd waved him off and gone to find something to pass the time with until he came back.

Elis kicks herself now, wishing she could have stopped him from going. A few weeks at most, that's what she'd thought when he'd left. Now, here she is, nearly three years later, still worrying daily whether or not he's still alive. She paces the house all day, not ever going out. Waiting. And when she's not waiting, she goes over their last conversation in her head, changing what she'd said so that he'd stay and wishing more than anything that she could change it for real.

Down the stairs and out into the garden she goes, to the bench at the back where she sits at times like this. When she can't stand the silence, she comes to sit here, where she's surrounded almost completely by plants and can lose herself listening to the night animals chattering. There are no clouds in the sky, so the moon and stars are the only source of light she has, but that makes it easier to pretend the world doesn't exist. Fireflies hang in the warm June air and crickets chirp from somewhere she can't see.

She remembers back to the first time she came out to sit here, watching the fireflies and listening to the crickets, and realising how relaxing it was. There were a whole different lot of insects then, and there would have been a completely new lot every couple of weeks. Elis must have seen thousands of bugs by now, but each of them will only have seen her. As the insects have grown old and died after living a full life, all she's done is sit here. Waiting.

She's still waiting now, although she doesn't know what for any more. She can practically feel time sliding past her, calmly but quickly, her chance to change things long gone and the chance to start again beginning to follow. She's older and a lot less attractive than when she met him, all the energy he fell in love with gone with him.

Maybe he took it on purpose.

A soft breeze sifts through the leaves and brings out goosebumps on her arms. As the leaves move, the faint light from the moon makes the shadows dance across the collection of moss and mud and dead plants which litter the floor. Whenever this happens she swears she sees something in the corner of her eye, but there's never anything when she turns to see. Today, though, she can see them right in front of her.

Coils of what looks like smoke slither across the ground, seeping in between the bushes and surrounding her feet. Elis can hear the whispers as the smoke crawls up the back of the bench she's sat on, almost as if it's trying to reach up to talk to her. Before long she can no longer see the bushes a few feet in front of her, and all she can hear is the whispers. At first they're so loud and there are so many she can't distinguish one from the other let alone work out what they're saying, but every now and then one of them is louder, and they all sound like him.

It's such a rare bird.

I can get it for you.

The voices hiss directly into her ears and send shivers rippling throughout her entire body. Elis stands up to leave but by now she's completely lost track of which way she was facing. Nothing but smoke in any direction; no change in shade or brightness to give her even a small clue as to which way she should go. She waves her arms around wildly but in vain, and all the while those stupid voices don't shut up.

I'll be back.

I'll bring the bird.

I promise I'll be okay.

I love you.

She stops, and so do the voices. Suddenly the world is silent, not even the chitchat of all the little critters that kept her company before. Only the silence and the intense screaming in her head that she came out here to ignore in the first place. Her eyes sting with a stab of realisation that he never said that last bit. In all the years they'd known each other he'd never once told Elis he loved her, no matter how many times she said it. Maybe everyone was right. Maybe it was just a teenage fling. Maybe he's not coming back - maybe . . .

He's found someone new already.

The thought of him having settled down and maybe even started a family while she sat here waiting for him brings down all the tears she's been holding back this whole time in one go. The smoky coils having retreated back to wherever they came from in the first place, she dashes across the patio to the house, slamming the door behind her.

He doesn't love you.

Sat on her bed Elis twirls the feather between her fingers, the tears having stopped by now. She doesn't see the point to them anyway; they won't help get him back, and she isn't even sad any more. She's just disappointed, but in herself, not him. She should have realised after the first year that he wouldn't come back. It's been too long, and now she's gone and wasted three years of her life, dreaming, fantasising. Waiting.

He never loved you.

She stands up suddenly, determined. Feather in hand, she leaves the house for the first time in what seems like a lifetime, and it feels amazing. The first thing she does is walk to the park they used to visit together when they first met and go to the tree under which they always sat. Elis finds a reasonably stiff stick and drives it into the ground next to the tree. She does this several times to loosen the soil, before scooping it all out and dumping it by the hole she's created.

In the hole, she places the feather, giving it one last glimpse of the world before covering it with soil until she can no longer see its blue, burying it along with her memories of him. This is her new beginning. She'll start her life again now, and go back to how she used to be before he left. She doesn't need him anyway. She never did.

•••

Amber sits at the dining table alone, facing his empty chair and fiddling with the small blue feather in her hands. It's been a month since he left, and she's sat like this countless times, wondering when the chair will be filled again. It's midnight and the house is dark, and she hates it. She hates being alone like this - it allows her to think and that's the last thing she wants to do. If she thinks, her mind conjures up all the horrible things that could have happened to him.

She thinks about the day he brought her the feather a lot, because it's not a painful memory and she can imagine feeling that happy again some day. *This feather is unique*, he'd said, and it had made her feel so special. He'd explained how each bird had one blue feather in its tail in amongst the black all over the rest of its body, and that was why it was so rare to find one. He'd told her they were nocturnal and only lived in some faraway place he couldn't remember the name of.

I could bring you one if you like.

Amber had been so happy, and she'd waved to him as he got into his car to leave. She remembers leaning down to the open window and kissing his cheek, whispering *I love you* in his ear. He'd smiled and promised he'd be okay, and that was that. She'd started waiting for him that day. But she'd found it was a lot harder to wait for something when you don't know the exact date, so time moved slower than it ever had before.

And now here she is, a month later, sitting by the dining table at midnight because she's unable to sleep.

Waiting.

Printed in Poland
by Amazon Fulfillment
Poland Sp. z o.o., Wrocław